HOOKED ON ⫶

Clandestine Affairs 5

Zara Chase

MENAGE EVERLASTING

Siren Publishing, Inc.
www.SirenPublishing.com

A SIREN PUBLISHING BOOK
IMPRINT: Ménage Everlasting

HOOKED ON A FEELIN'
Copyright © 2014 by Zara Chase

ISBN: 978-1-62741-909-3

First Printing: September 2014

Cover design by Les Byerley
All art and logo copyright © 2014 by Siren Publishing, Inc.

Printed in the U.S.A.

PUBLISHER
Siren Publishing, Inc.
www.SirenPublishing.com

HOOKED ON A FEELIN'

Clandestine Affairs 5

ZARA CHASE
Copyright © 2014

Chapter One

Raoul sat with his legs propped on the desk in front of him, his cowboy boots in danger of knocking expensive high-tech equipment to the floor. He was too unsettled to care. He and Zeke had just spent the day on horseback, helping the ranch hands to move stock to the summer pasture. He was physically tired, but mentally fucked. He didn't know what the hell the matter with him was.

Or rather he did.

Zeke opened a couple of bottles of beer and passed one to Raoul.

"Thanks, bud."

"No problem."

Zeke threw himself into the chair in front of Raoul's desk, upon which his feet joined Raoul's. Neither man said anything about the memories bugging them both as they made inroads into their beverages of choice. Anniversaries were always tough. In a few days' time it would be the third anniversary of the day when they had foolishly not stopped Cantara, Raoul's wife but the woman they both loved, from undertaking a doomed mission to help the Palestinian peace talks along. Raoul and Zeke, Special Forces Green Berets at the time, and supposedly the best there was—ha, what a joke—had barely escaped with their lives. Cantara had not been so lucky. Neither man had recovered, or found a way to move on. The shrinks would tell them it was cathartic to talk about it.

The shrinks didn't know shit.

"Wanna go into town tonight?" Zeke asked.

"Nah, things to do."

"I can see that."

Raoul sighed, removed his feet from the desk and pointedly logged onto his e-mail. Zeke shrugged and chugged back a swallow of beer without instigating any of the sarcastic banter that usually flew between them. Whoever said time was a great healer knew even less than the shrinks did about managing grief, loss and, most of all, guilt.

"Anything interesting?" Zeke asked, aware Raoul would he sifting through the usual pile of crap that came into their investigation agency on a daily basis.

"Same old, same old."

Raoul deleted one request after another, wondering how so many people got to hear about them, and what it was they thought they did. It was not as though they advertised their services. Marriage counsellors they were not, and yet half the US Armed Forces serving abroad seemed to want them to check up on erring spouses, off the rails teenagers, and other domestic disharmonies.

He was on the point of deleting the last message in his inbox when something gave him pause. They dealt with military personnel only, or their direct families, but something about the name Sorrel Lang rang a vague bell. Sorrel wasn't exactly a common name.

"Something?" Zeke asked, when Raoul sat forward and read the e-mail through for a second time.

"Not sure. Do you remember a Josh Lang? He was an army captain we came across when we were in Afghanistan, I think."

"Yeah, a good guy."

"Not anymore. Stepped on a land mine."

"Shit!"

"This is from his daughter, Sorrel. She says her dad copped it just over a year ago."

"That's tough. I'm surprised we didn't hear about it."

"Me too."

"Presumably she heard of us through her old man."

"Seems that way."

"What does she want?" Zeke asked, walking round the desk to read over Raoul's shoulder. "Advertising slogans?" He scratched his head. "She writes advertising slogans and someone's stealing them before she can pitch them. Industrial espionage ain't exactly our line."

"I liked her dad, so did you, and I do remember him talking a lot about his little girl. That's why the name stuck in my mind."

"Where is she?"

"In Seattle." Raoul leaned back in his chair and laced his fingers behind his head. "I guess it can't hurt to send someone to take a look-see, if we have anyone in the area."

"We do." Zeke had a photographic memory when it came to the location of their operatives—all ex-military in one guise or another—all disillusioned with the system and happy to work for the Clandestine Agency. As its name implied, the agency operated beneath the radar and its operatives administered their own brand of justice, without reference to the pen pushers or any rules other than those governing their own consciences. "Blaine and Dafoe are in Port Angeles. They run a fancy gym-cum-boot-camp down near the harbor."

"Right."

Raoul scrubbed a hand down his face as he Googled Sorrel's name. He found a professional-looking website proclaiming her to be an ad slogan writer of some renown. There were examples of her work, some witty enough to make Raoul chuckle, and testimonials from several established businesses in the Seattle area and beyond.

"She does designs to accompany her slogans," Zeke said, still peering over Raoul's shoulder. "A bit like individual logos for each campaign. That's kinda neat."

"Yeah, but I don't see any great mystery here. She's making a mark in a competitive field, which means she will have made enemies. Someone's obviously hacked her computer. She needs to get better online security, is all."

"Doesn't sound to me like she's that naïve. She wouldn't last long in advertising if she was. It's pretty cutthroat, by all accounts." Zeke straightened up and reapplied his attention to his beer. "Can't hurt to put the guys onto it. We owe it to her dad's memory to put her mind at rest."

"Yeah, I guess."

Raoul flipped through his phone contacts and called Blaine's cell.

* * * *

"Okay, guys, you did good. Now take five." A dozen sweat-drenched bodies fell to the ground, alternately sighing with relief, groaning, panting, and wiping brows. "Remember to rehydrate."

Vasco Blaine ran an eye over his motley collection of victims, just to reassure himself none were on the point of actually expiring. They came to the boot camp to be bullied into getting fit, learning to eat better and drop some weight, but it wouldn't be good for business if they died in the effort. An easy-paced three-mile jog around the Olympic National Forest on their third day of a two-week course had already sorted the men from the boys. Vasco knew that half these guys would drop out on one pretense or another before the course reached the halfway point. Their loss. They'd paid up front and *Body Language* had a no refund policy.

"Geez, Vasco," puffed one of the two women in the group—a forty-something divorcee in a tight Lycra top two sizes too small for her who could lose twenty pounds and never miss it. "I thought you said this would be fun."

Vasco flashed a smile, well aware what her idea of fun would be. She had been coming on to him and his partner Tyler since joining the course and was pretty thick-skinned when it came to taking *no* for an answer.

"This time next week you'll be able to cover that distance with ease, Lauren. That I can guarantee."

"If you say so, honey."

"It sure is pretty around here," one of the men remarked. "I'm starting to get all this communing with nature shit."

"Every activity you can think of is covered," Vasco replied.

Lauren's face lit up with a mischievous smile. Vasco was saved from the come-on line she was probably working up to when his cell phone rang. He was surprised to see Raoul's name flash on the display. It had been a while.

"Excuse me, guys," he said. "I need to take this."

Vasco wandered a little way away from his group and accepted the call.

"Hey, Raoul, what's up?"

"How you doin', Vasco?"

"Got fresh meat jogging around the forest."

Raoul laughed. "Sounds like fun."

"You have *no* idea." Vasco rolled his eyes. "Anyway, what can I do for you?"

Raoul explained he was forwarding an e-mail request for help from a lady in distress.

Vasco grinned. "My specialty."

Raoul's amused grunt echoed down the line. "How did I know you'd say that? Anyway, Zeke and I knew her old man. He didn't come back from 'Stan."

Vasco closed his eyes. "That's rough."

"Yeah well, I just sent Sorrel an e-mail and said you'd be in touch."

"Sorrel? That's a pretty name. Tyler and I will get right on it."

"I don't think it's a big deal, but let me know if there's anything in it, or if you need anything from me."

"Will do."

Vasco cut the call and returned to his group. Most of them had recovered sufficiently to at least sit up and bitch to one another about aching muscles. What the hell did they expect? Most of those muscles hadn't been used since before the invention of the wheel.

He was cautiously optimistic about the way the business he and Tyler had set up after getting out of the military was shaping up. Finances were tight and it would be several more years before they could hope to turn a profit on their investment. At the moment that was a very distant hope. There were a lot of other, well-established fitness emporiums in the area and they were having to offer crazy cheap deals to attract business away from the competition. Profit margins had been pared to the bone. If it didn't take off soon, they were sunk.

Vasco and Ty had put all their savings into the business, taken out a substantial business loan and negotiated subsidies from the city to get *Body Language* off the ground. They had jumped through all the necessary hoops and, overall, found it was a satisfying way to try and make a living. They felt they were making a difference, even if it had taught them more than they needed to know about the frailties of human nature.

They were both fitness freaks and felt something needed to be done to combat the slovenly eating and exercise habits of Joe Average. They quickly discovered that the lure of the gym with its state-of-the-art, ruinously expensive equipment wasn't enough to keep people involved once the first fit of enthusiasm faded. Even the offer of inexpensive personal trainers failed to keep members coming back once they realized exercise was hard work that required commitment and there was no fast-fix app to make it happen.

And so Vasco had the bright idea of the boot camp. They required clients to sign up for a full two-week initiation course. That meant taking time off work or, in some cases, being told to attend by employers concerned about their employees' sedentary lifestyles. It was early days but so far the course boasted a fifty percent graduation rate, which exceeded Vasco's expectations. A few of those graduates were now regular members of the gym, converted to the benefits of regular exercise, and with their bodies starting to show it.

In spite of their crazy busy days, trying to build on the initial success of their venture, which was now into its third year, and stave off a growing band of creditors, he and Ty still missed the buzz of being front line soldiers. Raoul was right. The cry for help he'd passed on didn't sound like any big deal, but they would check it out just the same and see if there was anything they could do to fix things.

"Okay, guys, let's get up on our feet, do a few stretches and make sure we're supple so we can jog back to the bus without injuring ourselves."

Groans and insults flew, but the group followed Vasco's lead and dutifully stretched their hamstrings, followed by a few gentle lunges and torso twists.

"Right, let's do it."

Vasco set an easy pace, not much faster than a brisk walk, and didn't break a sweat. His group, on the other hand, were soon strung out behind him in a straggling line, some of them really struggling. To their credit, they all made it back to the bus parked in the visitors' lot, even if they were again dripping and gasping for breath.

Lauren slid onto the seat beside him, pressed up against him way too close as Vasco drove the group back to the gym. He slammed on the brakes at one point to avoid rear-ending a truck that stopped dead in front of him. Lauren lurched even closer and slapped a large hand on his thigh.

"Sorry about that, guys."

Vasco steered around the now stationary truck, ignoring Lauren's hand until it crept dangerously close to ground zero. He shifted his position, forcing her to remove it without making a big deal out of it. He reminded himself of the size of their bank loan and fell back on charm and tact to fend off her suggestive remarks and increasingly determined efforts to pry into his private life. They needed these courses to work, and Lauren's employer had already sent several clients their way. She was something important in the managing partner's office and he needed her to return to work with glowing reports about *Body Language*. Her company was on the up and up, but didn't have gym facilities of its own. Vasco lived in hope of selling them on the idea of corporate membership before any of the competition got in ahead of him. To do that, he had to keep Lauren sweet.

Shit, he hadn't realized what was involved when he and Ty had what they thought was a simple business plan to open a fitness center.

"You did good, guys," Vasco said as they poured through the back door to the gym, some of them still out of breath. This group was going to be a challenge. "Now hit the showers, and make sure you have your menu suggestions for tonight. No cheating. I will know if you do. Just remember, all the exercise in the world won't do you much good if you don't think about what you put into your bodies, too. Any questions?" Mercifully there were none. "Okay, we'll see you tomorrow morning, nine sharp."

"What do you do for fun in the evenings?" Lauren asked, hanging back when the others took themselves off to the bathrooms.

"I'm booked out with classes," he lied.

"Shame." She winked at him. "All work and no play is as unproductive as empty calories."

"You could well be right. But now, if you'll excuse me."

"Oh, sure. I'll catch you later."

Vasco went in search of his partner, whom he found in the office.

"Hey, Ty."

Tyler looked up from a pile of invoices he was gloomily working his way through, probably deciding which ones could be ignored for a little longer. "Our insurance premiums have gone up by twenty frigging percent. Can you believe that?"

"Why?"

Ty shrugged. "Fucked if I know. Something about increased public liability."

"Because that idiot last year tried to lift weights that were way too heavy for him and then threatened to sue?"

"Most likely. Anyway, we'll have to shop around for something cheaper, I guess." Ty leaned back in his chair and stretched his arms above his head. "How did it go?"

"No one died. They just think they did."

Ty chuckled. "Always an encouraging outcome."

"We got a call from Raoul."

Ty discarded the invoices with a speed that belied any real conviction for bookkeeping. Neither of them was into paperwork, but they just couldn't afford to pay another employee to take it on, so they had to juggle it themselves, along with everything else. Good job neither of them needed much sleep to get by. "Anything interesting?"

"Hard to say." Vasco filled him in on what little he knew.

"Well, let's give the lady a call. Raoul wouldn't have passed her problem to us if he really thought it was nothing."

"Sounds like a plan."

Vasco threw himself into the chair behind his own desk and picked up the phone.

Chapter Two

Sorrel nibbled the end of her pen, racking her brains for a phrase to make toilet cleaner sound sexy and dynamic. As if toilet cleaner wasn't enough of a challenge, the brand name was even worse. *Bubblebowl.* She giggled as all sorts of inappropriate connotations occurred to her. Uh-huh! She shook her head and adjured herself to concentrate, but her mind remained blank. No, that wasn't true. Her mind was buzzing with too much other stuff for her to be able to focus on what she did best. The demands on her time, attention and, most of all, her recently inherited money, seemed limitless. Who said you couldn't buy popularity, she wondered, rolling her eyes before sighing and doing her very best to get her creative juices flowing.

Zilch.

Perhaps a little fresh air would clear out all the junk rattling around inside her brain. She whistled to Marley, the small, wiry black and white stray mutt she had acquired in the way she appeared to be acquiring stray humans recently. Marley had followed her in the park for several days in a row, looking half-starved, near frozen to death and totally irresistible with one ear pointing skyward and the other flat against his head. On day four she gave in and took him home with her. He was proving to be great, undemanding company, as well as unfailingly loyal, and had never given her cause to regret her decision.

"Come on, buddy, let's stretch our paws."

Marley jumped off the armchair he had been stretched out in and wagged his entire body. Before she could grab his leash her doorbell rang, and ignoring it wasn't an option, tempting though the prospect was. She wasn't expecting anyone, and whoever it was, she probably didn't want to see them. But she still couldn't pretend not to be at home. Because she worked from her apartment, her family and friends seemed to think she was available twenty-four-seven. She tried explaining that she wouldn't dream of calling upon them in their offices in the middle of the working day and expect them to drop everything, but received only uncomprehending stares for her efforts. Sighing, she pulled the door open, Marley yapping around her heels, and her heart plummeted when she found herself face to face with Jordi, her ex. He held a wilting bunch of roses and wore a puppy dog smile. Sorrel had prayed for this moment for weeks after he dumped her. Now her prayers had been answered and she waited for joy to grip her.

All she felt was…well, annoyance.

"Hey, babe, not interrupting anything, am I?"

"Actually, you are. I was just on my way out."

Jordi ignored her, thrust the flowers into her hands and pushed past her into the apartment. Marley growled at him, but Jordi either didn't notice, or chose to ignore the frosty reception he received from both dog and its owner.

"I thought we could grab some dinner."

"It's four thirty in the afternoon."

"Early bird special. I need to go into work later."

Cheapskate. He was a celebrity chef in a top-end restaurant but wanted to palm her off with a cheap, fast meal. And not so long ago, she would have been pathetically grateful for the attention.

"I think you got the wrong address. We don't date anymore." His smile widened, infuriating Sorrel. "We broke up."

He flapped a hand. "Aw, that was nothing."

"You never wanted to see me again."

"We were stagnating. We needed a break for a while."

Anger surged through Sorrel. Where had he been when she had needed him so badly? The fact that he seemed convinced he would be welcomed back with open arms told her that, like her family, he just assumed he could push her around because she had always allowed it.

Not anymore.

"Now, let me see if I remember this right." She canted her head and rested her chin in her splayed hand. "I'm narrow-minded, cramped your style, clung, and what else was it? Oh yes, I was fat."

"I did not say you were fat."

No, but you implied it. "So what's changed?"

But Sorrel already knew. Her father's will had been probated, and she'd gotten the lion's share. Her parents had divorced several years previously, and Mom had received a very fair settlement at that time. Her brother and sister had constantly gone to Dad, hands outstretched for help with their latest wild projects, none of which flourished. Only Sorrel had wanted nothing from him other than his unconditional love. One year after his death, she still seldom got through a day without crying for the loss of him.

Dad, bless his heart, had made good on his promise to Sorrel and ensured her siblings' greed was reflected in the final distribution of his inherited family wealth. Pete and Maggie had been stunned, and complained long and loud about the unfairness of it all, conveniently forgetting that they had already received more than Sorrel finished up with. Dad thought he was doing her a favor. He couldn't have realized the squabbles and bad feeling his thoughtfulness would create.

Jordi had broken her already shattered heart when, at the time of her dad's death, instead of being there for her, he took up with one of her so-called friends, claiming Sorrel had let herself go. That it coincided with him being headhunted for a top chef's job in a chic restaurant hadn't escaped her notice. Presumably, looking as though she enjoyed his food a little too much was bad for business. But now her appearance had improved, along with her bank balance.

"Look, babe, can't we at least be friends?"

"No, it's not genetically possible for single, heterosexual men and women to be *friends.*"

"Who told you that?"

Sorrel waved the question aside. "It's a well-known fact."

She waited for him to ask about Marley. She hadn't owned him at the time of their break up. He didn't, but Marley continued to growl at him. *Good dog!*

"Okay then, if we can't be friends, let's be business partners."

Here it comes. "Why?"

"Why?"

Jordi looked like he didn't understand the question. Sorrel watched him as he struggled for words, wondering what the attraction had been. He was fun, she'd give him that, as well as being popular and was quite good looking. Everyone told her he was a catch and she was lucky to have him, so she believed it. Now she saw a weak, vacuous man, and figured he'd done her a favor by ending the relationship. If they'd still been an item when her dad's money had come through, she would have been vulnerable, leaning on him for support, and he would soon have talked her into parting with it.

"Yes, Jordi, why? Why would you want me for a partner? I know absolutely nothing about the catering business."

"You don't need to. I know all there is to know."

That was a stretch but still, for all his faults, Jordi was an excellent chef.

"I'm going into business on my own. Opening my own restaurant."

"Congratulations."

He seemed taken aback by her lack of enthusiasm. When they had been together, she would have thrown herself into his arms, told him how clever he was, how convinced she felt that his venture would succeed, and encouraged him to go for it. Now, she couldn't give a damn what he did, just so long as he didn't think he would get to do it with her money.

"Is that all you can say?"

She shrugged. "What would you have me say?"

"Listen, darlin', just take a look at this." He handed her a sheaf of papers. "These are the premises I plan to take in a really good location, start-up costs, projected profits, the works. Once you see what a good investment it is, you'll trip over yourself to get involved."

"If it's such a surefire thing, why involve someone else?"

She folded her arms beneath her admittedly oversized breasts and sent him a look of innocent enquiry. Like he wasn't at least the fourth person to try and tap her for a loan since her dad's will had been published. Did they really think she was that naïve? Jordi had good reason to, she supposed. She had been pathetically grateful to call him a boyfriend, but that was in another life. Once she got over him she decided she was better off flying solo, rather than getting her heart trampled on by someone else. There was nothing a man could give her that her vibrator couldn't make a much better job of. Admittedly, it only had Jordi to compete against, which probably wasn't saying much, but still…

"Sorry. I'm not with you."

"Why not just go to the bank and ask for a loan?"

"I could do that, but I wanted to give you an opportunity to get in on the ground floor."

"Seriously?"

"Yeah, I thought you'd be pleased," he said smugly.

Arrogant bastard! "That's real kind of you, Jordi, but I think I'll pass, thanks."

"Pete's on board."

Sorrel flexed a brow. "What, my brother? That Pete?" Now this was starting to make sense. "I had no idea you guys kept in touch."

"Our paths cross, being in the catering industry. Pete has great ideas for some signature cocktails to launch the restaurant. He'll run the bar, obviously."

Sorrel managed not to shudder. Unlike Sorrel, Pete and her sister Maggie were both tall, slim and beautiful, with acres of charisma, just like their mother. But Pete was hopelessly impractical. The money he had begged from their dad went to opening his own bar. It didn't survive the first year. Sorrel felt obliged to remind Jordi of that fact. Her ex was many things, most of them unpleasant, but he *was* an excellent chef and didn't deserve to have his dreams shattered by an impractical partner.

"Oh, Pete has learned from his mistakes," Jordi said airily.

"But he has no actual money to invest." Sorrel narrowed her eyes at her ex nearest and no longer dearest. "Did he suggest you talk to me? Is that what this is all about?"

Jordi looked sheepish. He had obviously expected Sorrel to fall all over him, and didn't know how to handle the new, improved, independent version. "Well, he did mention you might be interested."

She held the papers out to him. "Sorry, but it's not for me."

"Keep them." He looked and sounded a little desperate. "Read through them and we'll talk again when you've had a chance to think about it."

Don't hold your breath. Jordi tried to kiss her but she moved out of range.

"I'd really like it if we could get together again real soon."

I can't think why. "Thanks for dropping by," she said, opening the front door and standing back to let him pass through it.

"Later, babe."

Much later.

Sorrel didn't know whether to laugh or cry. But this time the tears would be caused by humor, not heartbreak. Everyone connected with her seemed to think she had just gotten off a banana boat. Yes, she'd inherited a lot of money, but not enough that she could give up working, or finance half the schemes of…well, of her scheming friends and relations.

Before she could pick up Marley's leash, her phone rang. Just like her doorbell, she found it impossible to ignore. It might be to do with work.

"Hey, darling."

Sorrel smothered a groan when she heard her mother's voice. She was well aware she was her mother's least favorite child. They had very little in common, Sorrel being much more like her father than her brother and sister. Mom and Maggie were walking fashion gurus. Sorrel glanced down at her overweight body and conceded she was more a fashion victim. Mom had been in touch with Sorrel more over the past few weeks than she had for years. Big surprise. She had run through her divorce settlement in less time than it took Marley to chase his ball across the park. She had failed to retain the interest of the wealthy entrepreneur whom she had left Dad for, and was now constantly on the lookout for someone to finance her high-maintenance lifestyle.

"Hi, Mom. I was just on my way out the door."

"I've been reading about this amazing new cruise line. We really ought to try it, darling. It sound divine. And the accommodations are just to die for. We could go next month."

"Is it expensive?" Sorrel asked out of curiosity. She was interested to know how much her mother expected to take her for this time.

"Oh no, it's really amazingly cheap."

Uh-huh. Sorrel's mom didn't do cheap. "Well then, I really think you should go."

"I'm so pleased, darling. I could book—"

"I'm sure your friend Molly would like to go with you."

Sorrel was being a bitch, which was most unlike her, but she couldn't help herself. She'd had enough of being taken for a fool. She wasn't supposed to know it because Mom would find it too embarrassing to admit to her failure, but Maggie had told her in a rare moment of sisterly solidarity—make that sucking up—that Molly was the reason why Mom was newly single. Molly had snitched the eligible entrepreneur from right under Mom's nose.

"Molly's busy right now," she said curtly. "I thought you and I could go, darling. When did we last take a vacation together?"

When did you last take an interest in me? "No can do, Mom. I have a job, remember."

"Oh, but you can do that from anywhere."

"No." Sorrel gritted her teeth. "Actually, I can't."

"Well look, don't decide now. I'll e-mail you the details. I'm sure you'll change your mind once you see them."

Sorrel managed to get off the phone without committing herself to the floating nightmare, but it rang again almost immediately.

"I am not going to answer it," she told Marley, who sat with head cocked to one side, patiently waiting for his walk. "I'm absolutely not."

Marley whined his agreement.

"Yes." Sorrel snatched up the phone, furious with herself for being unable to break the habit of a lifetime. She only hoped for their sakes it wasn't her sister or brother, asking for yet another favor.

"Is that Sorrel Lang?"

Someone trying to sell her something. That was all she needed.

"Yes, but I'm not buying," she said with what, for her, was bluntness that bordered on being downright rude.

"I'm not selling." The amused, rich masculine voice on the other end of the phone made her insides curl and her regret being so curt. It was the sort of voice that wrapped itself around its listener like a sexy comfort blanket. Could blankets be sexy? *Stop it, Sorrel. You're not working now.* "Vasco Blaine. Raoul Washington asked me to call."

"Oh God!" Sorrel clapped a hand over her mouth. "I'm sorry for being so brusque."

"Bad day, huh?"

"You have no idea."

"I hear you have a problem."

"Yes, you see—"

"Not over the phone. You're in downtown Seattle, right?"

"Yes, but I have a car. I can meet you somewhere."

"My partner and I have business your way this evening. Let's meet in person and talk about this." Vasco named a small, little-known restaurant that just happened to be a favorite of hers. She took that to be the first positive sign in an otherwise shitty day. "Do you know where it is?"

Sorrel did, obviously. It was off the beaten track, family run, cheap and good value, so not a hang-out for the beautiful people keen to be seen. Which meant it suited Sorrel perfectly. Jordi had always spoke of it with disdain. They agreed to meet there in two hours' time.

"Well, Marley," she told the dog, suddenly feeling much better. "That's a turn up for the books. Someone wanting to do something for *me* for a change. Come on, sweetness, we're going to meet a silver-tongued guy who will probably be a huge disappointment in the flesh." She rolled her eyes. "But what do we care, right?"

Chapter Three

Vasco and Tyler arrived early at the restaurant and sat at the bar, drinking light beers while they waited for a table to free up. They'd been there less than five minutes when a young woman of average height, with a scruffy little dog on a leash, appeared in the doorway. She scanned the bar, briefly looked at the pair of them and as quickly looked away again.

"Is that her, do you suppose?" Tyler asked.

"Could be." Vasco continued to watch her. "She didn't seem too impressed by us. Barely spared us a glance."

Tyler chuckled. "You've got so used to females coming on to you at the gym, and just about everywhere else for that matter, that you've forgotten how to take rejection."

Vasco grinned. "Ain't had much experience at rejection."

"Not too hot on modesty, either."

Vasco waved Ty's comment aside, still taking inventory of the woman and liking what he saw. She wore faded jeans and a long, loose top, obviously designed to hide the fact that she carried a little extra weight around her middle. It couldn't hide her large tits, or equally large backside, but Vasco wasn't complaining. Just because he toned bodies for a living, didn't mean he couldn't appreciate nature at her finest. This creature carried her extra weight well, mainly because her posture was good, and because she wasn't trying to flaunt her assets by wearing tight clothing.

She had a waterfall of natural brunette hair, held back with a clip, and an averagely pretty face with slightly jutting cheekbones, rendered interesting by the most remarkable greenish-silver eyes. She wore no makeup as far as Vasco could detect, and didn't need to. He approved of her creamy, fresh-faced, natural look almost as much as he approved of her full, sensual mouth and delicate, symmetrical features.

"I like," Tyler said, giving her a third look.

She still didn't appear to have found whomever she expected to meet, so Vasco took a chance.

"Sorrel?" he asked, standing up and beckoning.

She looked at him like he'd spoken in a foreign language. Her eyes widened with considerable caution, like they had ax murderers tattooed on their chests, and didn't move for a prolonged moment. The hostess approached her with a smile, which snapped her out of her indecision and she politely focused her attention of the restaurant employee.

"Is it okay to bring the dog into the bar area?" she asked. "He's well behaved…well, most of the time."

"That's fine, honey," the hostess replied. "But you can't take him in the restaurant. Are you meeting someone?"

"These guys, I think," she said, gesturing towards Vasco and Tyler.

The hostess looked astounded. "You mean you don't actually know?"

"No, but I'm about to find out. Wish me luck."

Sorrel walked across to them. Vasco and Tyler stood as she approached and shared a look, impressed by the natural grace and coordination of her movements. Vasco noticed a few men in the restaurant area look up as she passed, probably thinking the same thing.

"She has possibilities," Tyler muttered. "Think she's one of us?"

"If she is, she doesn't know it yet."

"Well, I can teach her all she needs to know."

"This is work. Down boy."

"Too late for that. She's gotten to me already," Tyler replied, unabashed.

Vasco shook his head, then extended his hand as Sorrel reached them "Hey, Sorrel. I'm Vasco Blaine. We spoke earlier."

"Hi." Her small hand disappeared into his much larger one and Vasco held it there, in no hurry to release it. "It's nice to meet you."

"I'm Tyler Dafoe."

Vasco let her hand go so Tyler could literally get to grips with it. "Nice to meet you too," she said, in a low, husky voice. "I only hope I haven't dragged you here under false pretenses."

"No worries. We were in town anyway," Vasco said. "Who's this guy?"

"Oh, that's Marley. He's a stray who adopted me a while back. Now we're joined at the hip."

Both men bent to pet the friendly little dog, who lapped up the attention as enthusiastically as he lapped at their hands. Sorrel slipped onto a bar stool between the two of them and the bartender immediately appeared with a bowl of water for the dog.

"Thank you," Sorrel said, smiling. "That's very thoughtful of you."

"We take good care of all our customers," the bartender replied, winking at her.

"What would you like to drink, Sorrel?" Vasco asked.

Before she could reply, the hostess walked up to them. "Excuse me, but if you want to eat in the bar, there's a table free. It means you can keep the dog with you."

"Sounds like a plan." Vasco smiled at the hostess, who blushed. "Thanks, honey. Lead the way."

Once they were seated, with Sorrel between them and the dog beneath the table, the hostess left them menus and the bartender came over again and took Sorrel's drink order. She asked for a diet soda.

"I'm trying to lose a few pounds," she explained self-consciously.

"Actually, you don't need to lose much," Tyler said, smiling as he gave her a probing look that made her blush.

"Excuse me?"

"We run a gym," Vasco explained, "which makes us think we're experts on the subject."

"Oh, in Seattle?"

"Port Angeles. It's called *Body Language.* "

"Oh, I've heard good things about it. I know someone who's a member, but I've never set foot in a gym. I'm allergic to exercise." She laughed self-consciously and indicated her body with her hands. "As you can see. Well, I do walk. I have no choice now that I have this little guy, but I did before I got him, too. It's my thinking time, if I get stuck with a slogan. Still, I don't suppose walking really counts as exercise."

"Actually, regular fast walking is one of the best forms of aerobic exercise," Vasco told her.

"Oh, is it?" She looked pleased. "Well, I have dropped a few pounds since getting Marley, so perhaps you're right. Mind you, I could do with losing more yet, as my mother and sister never tire of reminding me."

"Ty's right about you, even if he is outspoken to the point of rudeness. You just need to tone up a bit and you'll be dynamic."

Her blush deepened. "Thank you. I think."

Vasco chuckled. "No problem."

"Sorrel's an unusual name," Ty said. "Something to do with herbs, isn't it?"

"Yes, but Sorrel's a pretty ordinary herb, actually." She shrugged. "A bit like me. It's been cultivated for centuries and used in soups and salads, stuff like that."

"I guess you get that question a lot," Vasco said, smiling at her.

She nodded. "Yeah, I do."

"Well, it's a pretty name and it suits you."

And if you say you're not pretty, I shall put you across my knee and spank you. Vasco couldn't remember the last time he'd found a woman who was so unsure of herself and wondered who had knocked all the confidence out of her. Nowadays females were all so damned predatory it spoiled the thrill of the chase. Who wanted to pursue a woman who allowed herself to be easily caught?

She blushed at the compliment and looked down at her hands. "Thanks."

They turned their attention to the menus. Vasco watched her while she considered her options, trying to get a handle on her. Ty was right. She was sensual, but she was also self-conscious about her body, and had probably never had a chance to find that out about herself. Shame. She struck him as a responsible, giving person, who put others before herself. After all, she'd taken in a stray dog because she felt sorry for the little guy, which said a lot about her.

A server came to take their order. Both guys ordered steaks. Vasco thought Sorrel would probably like one too, but she ordered a chicken Caesar instead.

"We were sorry to hear about your dad," Tyler said when the server left them.

"Thank you." She swallowed. "Did you know him? You're obviously ex-military yourselves."

"We were marines, and no we didn't know him," Vasco said. "But Raoul and Zeke did and they speak highly of him."

"Thanks again." She looked on the verge of tears, which told Vasco that she and her father had been close. It had been a year since her father's passing and she still got emotional at the mention of his name. "That means a lot." She paused. "Dad told me Raoul was married to a Palestinian lady, but that she died. Is that right?"

"Yes, but I'm surprised your dad knew. It was confidential because she worked for the US and Israel, trying to broker peace. She got killed on a mission—"

"That's so sad."

"Yeah, it was about three years ago. Raoul and Zeke got out of the military just after that and set up their investigation agency. They have people like us all over the country, ready to step in and help where it's needed."

"I can understand why he would want to do that," she said, idly fiddling with a salad fork. "No one could help his wife, but he might be able to help others."

"Right," Ty said. "And talking of help, tell us about your problems."

"Well, now that I'm here, I'm not really sure that I actually have one."

"You must have thought you did, otherwise you wouldn't have contacted Raoul. And he must have agreed, otherwise we wouldn't be here. He gets dozens of requests every week and is very selective about the ones he takes further."

"Oh, I didn't realize."

"You write advertising slogans?" Vasco asked.

"Yes, and I design logos to go with each campaign. I thought that idea up myself, just to make me stand out from the competition. Now almost everyone does it."

"Do you work for an agency?" Ty asked.

"No, I work freelance but some agencies do ask me for ideas sometimes. I've earned a bit of a reputation, you see, and have quite a broad client base."

Vasco suspected she was being modest. She didn't strike him as the type to boast about her achievements. "Does slogan writing pay well?" he asked.

"Not especially, but if your slogan is adopted, there's every chance you'll be asked to work on the campaign. That's where the real money is."

"I see."

"Recently several of my ideas have been pitched to the clients, almost word for word, before I could submit them myself. At first I thought it was coincidence." She shrugged. "I mean, when you're talking just a short, snappy slogan based around the name of a product, it's possible for several people to come up with the same idea, I suppose. Unlikely, but not impossible."

"But it happened enough for you to start thinking someone was actually stealing from you?" Ty suggested.

"Yes, because my logo designs turned up as well."

Their food arrived, looking and smelling great. Vasco ordered a bottle of red and insisted that Sorrel take a glass. If nothing else, it might help her to relax.

"Well, just one won't kill my resolve, I guess."

"Presumably you do your designing and brainstorming by computer," Ty said as he cut into his rare steak and blood oozed over the plate. "Hmm, this is good."

"The food's always good here," Sorrel said, glancing rather enviously at their plates.

"You come here a lot?" Vasco asked.

"Not as often as I'd like to. My family don't think it's trendy enough to bother with, nor does my ex."

"Good enough reason to be an ex," Ty remarked.

"Hmm, anyway, about my designs. Hell no, I don't use a computer. I know how easily they can be hacked, especially in such a cutthroat business as advertising." A flash of anger passed through her eyes, presumably because they hadn't credited her with more sense. "If you thought I'd called you in on a simple case of computer fraud, then I've wasted your time."

"Sorry," Vasco said. "But we needed to be sure. So, how do you work?"

She smiled at them both, an uncontrived, natural gesture that illuminated her eyes and banished the anxiety that had been in her expression ever since she walked in. Vasco's interest in her heightened. So did his cock. Shit, that was so inappropriate! There was just something about her that got to him, and he was already hooked on the feeling. Perhaps it was because she hadn't once tried to flirt with either of them, which was unusual enough to get their attention. It was as though she didn't think she was worthy of their regard, which was just plain dumb.

"The old fashioned way," she replied. "With pen and paper. I think better if I doodle at the same time and doodling on a screen just isn't the same."

"So someone who has access to your apartment must be—"

Her cell phone rang. She appeared annoyed by the interruption but pulled it from her pocket and checked the display. She rejected the call and turned her attention back to Vasco.

"Sorry about that. You were saying."

"Do you live alone?"

"Yes. Well, apart from Marley."

Upon hearing his name, the dog looked up hopefully and thumped his tail against the wooden floor, probably driven crazy by the aroma of steak.

"Anyone else have keys?" Ty asked.

Once again her cell rang.

"Oh, for goodness sake! Excuse me, but he won't give up until I take this. I'll just be a moment."

Vasco expected her to leave the table for privacy but she didn't, presumably because of the dog.

"Yes, Pete, what do you want?" She listened. "No, you can't. I'm not home right now." Another pause. "None of your business where I am. Besides, I'm mad at you. What the devil did you think you were doing, sending Jordi around?" Pause. "No, I don't and no I won't. It's a crazy idea and I want no part of it."

She cut the call, looking angry and upset. "Sorry, that was my brother, thinking he can push me around, like always." She took a large sip of wine. Vasco picked up the bottle and topped off her glass. She looked like she could use it. "Where were we? Oh yes, keys to my apartment. The super has one, obviously, and I think my sister does."

"What about the ex you mentioned?"

"Shit!" She covered her mouth with her hand. "Sorry, I'd forgotten. He does, but I can't see him stealing my ideas."

"Do you know who sold the ideas to the clients?"

"Obviously not. If I did—"

"You wouldn't need us." Vasco nodded. "Was it an amicable split from your ex?"

"No. He dumped me and I was devastated at the time, but I got over him."

Ty touched her hand, probably sensing that she was more upset than she was letting on. "How long ago was this?"

"A year."

"He dumped you at the same time you lost your dad?" Vasco shook his head. "What a jerk. Sounds like you're better off without him."

"It was just after Dad died. He seemed to think I was spending too much time grieving and not enough fanning his ego."

"Sounds like a real charmer." Ty growled.

"Well, I suppose part of what he said was true. I eat too much when I'm unhappy and he said I'd let myself go, which I suppose I had."

Vasco's desire to spank some sense into her intensified by the minute. "It was *not* your fault," he said softly, fixing her with a probing gaze. "And Ty's right. Again. That's twice in one day, which, I gotta tell you, is a rarity."

His quip produced the smile he'd been hoping for. "Jordi actually did me a favor, but it was a tough time and it took a while for me to see it that way."

"And he still has a key?" Ty asked.

"Yeah, I'll get the locks changed." She shook her head. "I should have thought of that before and not bothered you. Sorry."

"It's no bother, honey." Vasco smiled at her, badly wanting to banish the bruised, disillusioned look in her eye. "And if you're right and your ex wouldn't know how to go about flogging your ideas, it must be a rival."

"I agree, but…damn!"

Her cell rang again. She shrugged at them both and took the call. "Maggie, what can I do for you?" Pause. "Orlando? Why on earth would I want to go there?" Another pause. "The kids want to go, so take them. Don't expect me to drag along. Oh, or is it that you just expect me to pay?" Another pause. "What else am I supposed to think? We're not exactly tight." Pause. "This weekend? I'm not sure if I can. You'll have to let me get back to you on that one. I'm not at home right now." Pause. "No, I'm not with Jordi. Why on earth would I be?"

She sighed and broke the connection. This time she switched her phone off. "I don't often turn it off," she said, "just in case it's a work enquiry, but I've had quite enough of my family for one day."

"That was your family?" Ty asked.

"My sister. She wants me to pay for a weekend at Orlando for her and her kids *and* have the kids this weekend while she goes off somewhere with her new boyfriend."

"You must be a very loving aunt," Vasco said.

Sorrel shuddered. "Hardly. Her kids are monsters. Undisciplined, rude, demanding, but I never seem able to say *no* to Maggie. She guilts me into helping her."

"What do you have to feel guilty about?" Vasco asked, slipping his hand beneath the table and feeding Marley a sneaky piece of steak.

"You shouldn't do that," she said, with no real conviction in her tone.

"Poor guy looked hungry."

Sorrel laughed. "It's a look he's perfected when he recognizes a soft touch."

"Well, he's found one." Vasco reached down to ruffle the dog's ears. "I always had dogs as a kid. I miss having one around."

"I know just what you mean. My family thought I was mad when I took Marley in. They just don't realize what good company dogs can be. They give unconditional love, and the only demands they make in return are for food and exercise. Seems like a pretty good deal to me."

The server interrupted to clear their plates.

"You didn't answer my question about your guilt tendencies," Vasco reminded her when they were alone again. "Or rather, you skilfully avoided it."

"Right now my thoughts are on the dessert menu, and that's enough to make me feel riddled with guilt." She grinned. "The desserts here are to die for, and I'll die before my time if I keep stuffing myself with empty calories."

"Seems to me this is an emergency, so the normal rules don't apply." Ty signaled to the server. "One large portion of triple layer chocolate cake, please, and three forks."

"Don't!" Sorrel groaned, closing her eyes for an expressive minute, fanning her cheeks with thick, curling lashes. "That's my very favorite, but you guys are obviously fitness fanatics and ought to be setting a good example."

"We'll help you with it, darlin'," Vasco said. "But in return, you need to be completely honest with us."

"Deal," she said, grinning.

Chapter Four

"What do you need to know?" Sorrel asked.

"Tell us about your family," Ty replied. "They seem to play a big part in your life."

Sorrel took a moment to assimilate her thoughts, reminding herself to breathe, and at the same time wanting to pinch herself. That she was here with these two fine specimens of male physicality, and holding their attention, was surreal. They were drop-dead gorgeous and had every female head in the establishment swiveling in their direction so frequently she'd be surprised if the restaurant didn't get sued for multiple cases of whiplash. And they weren't just playing nice. They really seemed to want to help her. They actually cared. No one had cared about her, really cared, since her dad had passed. Even then, he was abroad so often with his unit that she hadn't liked to bother him with her problems when he was at home.

"My mom and dad divorced several years before Dad died," she said, making an effort to keep her emotions in check. "Dad was devastated, but she's high maintenance and didn't like being left at home all the time while he was off risking his life for his country."

"It happens more than you might think," Vasco said, sympathy in his tone.

"Well, I tried to convince Dad he was better off without her, and I think he started to see things that way when it came to divorce time and she showed her true colors. Anyway, I also have an older brother, who works as a bartender, and the sister with two kids who's divorced and works at being a pain in the neck." Sorrel sighed. "Not that she has to work too hard at that. She's got it down to a fine art already."

"I get that you were close to your dad, but not so much the rest of your family."

She grinned at Vasco, who had made the comment. "Nothing gets past you."

The dessert arrived, and it was all Sorrel could do not to drool at the sight of it. Vasco grinned, took a forkful and held it to her lips.

"Eat!" he commanded.

"So bossy," she muttered, but she swallowed the forkful of cake, closed her eyes and savored the sweet taste on her tongue, holding it there before slowly chewing and letting it slide down her throat. "Orgasmic! Better than sex."

The two guys laughed. "Honey, if that's what you think, you've been doing it all wrong," Ty said.

"Or doing it with the wrong person," Vasco added.

"That, too."

"Don't interrupt me while I'm salivating," Sorrel said, still with her eyes closed.

"Here you go, babe."

It was Ty this time who offered her a forkful of cake, and she was powerless to resist. She would definitely get back onto her eating plan tomorrow, she promised herself, but it would take more willpower than she would ever possess to resist this divine cake. She opened her eyes again and licked chocolate cream from her lips with the tip of her tongue. She noticed the guys share a look. It seemed liked they were in pain and she wondered what she'd done wrong. They were probably disgusted with her greed, she thought, blushing and hastily picking up her napkin to wipe her mouth.

Before she knew it the plate was empty and, to her mortification, she suspected she was responsible for that situation. Once she got started, she couldn't seem to stop, and she hadn't noticed the guys eat any of it.

"Better?" Vasco asked, grinning at her.

"Now I *really* feel guilty."

"Then stick to sex, honey," Ty said, winking at her. "Presumably that doesn't make you feel guilty."

Perhaps not, but the thoughts running through her head at that precise moment sure as hell did. Not guilt, but regret. She regretted not having the physical attributes to make an impression upon either of them. Such thoughts didn't normally creep up on her but, hey, she was only human.

She eyed the two guys who had answered her cry for help, still figuring her overactive imagination was playing tricks on her, hating that she was wasting their time over nothing. Vasco was all of six two. He had thick dirty-blond hair that fell across his eyes whenever he moved his head. The compulsion to reach forward and push it aside was…well, compelling. His rugged features were so artistically angled, so complimentary of one another, there really ought to be a law against it. He had a day's worth of stubble on his chin that only added to the draw she felt toward him. The compassion, the kindness, in his silver-gray eyes would make it easy to confide in him. His looks, his build, ought to make him self-centered, maybe even arrogant. Instead, he appeared to be a genuinely nice person. Go figure.

Even so, she reminded herself to be on her guard. She was no longer the naïve little girl who saw nothing but kindness and good in the world. She knew people were lining up to exploit her, with her family at the head of the queue. Part of her wondered if that's why these two were still here. They didn't seem to think she had a problem worthy of their talents, so what did she have that they did want? She dismissed the idea as unworthy. She might no longer be naïve, but she hadn't developed a cynical edge quite yet, had she?

Ty was Vasco's polar opposite in that his hair was shorter, darker, his eyes a deep chocolate brown. They were both muscle-bound hunks, disturbingly poised and yet at ease with themselves and the world in general. Unless anyone ticked them off. If that happened Sorrel guessed they would make intimidating adversaries. Hard, taut bodies flowing with masculine power, handsome faces, and lazy persuasive charm vied with an overall impression of raw power and sexual magnetism. Sorrel's body woke up from its sex-free extravaganza and took a keen interest in her dinner companions, even though she wasn't stupid enough to imagine her interest could ever be reciprocated.

"Okay, so you don't get on with your family, and I get the impression from listening to you on the phone that they resent you in some way." Vasco fixed her with an intense gaze that made her feel naked, but in a good way. "Am I right?"

"Yeah, I guess."

"And your ex?" Ty added. "I'm guessing he's the Jordi you mentioned. Where does he figure in your recent problems?"

She sighed, knowing she would have to tell them, trust them, if they were to help her. "Okay, you might as well know that Dad left me well provided for. His family had money that he inherited and passed on to me."

"He didn't include your brother and sister?" Ty asked.

"They kept going to him before he died. He gave them a shedload of cash, all of which they blew on stupid schemes that didn't pay. He also gave Mom a generous settlement when they divorced, way more than she deserved, but she's gone through that already. He promised he'd make it up to me when he died, and he did."

"But your siblings and mother think that's not fair."

Sorrel blew air through her lips. "That's about the size of it. Maggie keeps banging on about her kids, saying how it isn't right no provision was made for them, when she could have done something for them herself when Dad funded her last doomed enterprise. Now she wants to start a beauty parlor and expects me to finance it." Sorrel sighed. "Dad backed her previous effort, which tanked, and yet she still thinks she can make her mark as a businesswoman."

"A lot of people think that way, until they discover the realities," Ty said.

Sorrel sent him a curious glance, wondering if he was speaking from experience. "Anyway, don't get me started on my mom. Her latest wheeze is to try and get us to go on a cruise together, presumably because it's a good hunting ground for single males." She grinned. "Short of jumping overboard, they have no escape. But honestly, guys, can you see me on a cruise ship?"

"You couldn't pay me to get on one of those floating gin palaces," Vasco said, scowling.

"Me neither. Mom and Maggie are tall and slim and attractive, and love being the center of attention. In other words, they're all the things I'm not and never will be."

"Stop putting yourself down, sweetheart," Ty said softly. "Do you hear Vasco and me complaining about being seen with you?"

"You have no choice. You offered to help and I'm paying you." She clapped a hand over her mouth. "Oh God, sorry! That came out all wrong. I am so not good at taking compliments. No practice, you see."

"We'll have to do something about that," Vasco said, his eyes burning with an unfathomable emotion that made her blush.

"We've never had much in common before, Mom, Maggie and me, that is," Sorrel continued hastily, hoping she wasn't blushing quite as furiously as she thought she was. "But now they won't leave me alone." She closed her eyes for an expressive moment. "I know what they're doing to me, and why, and I know I shouldn't let it get to me. But, well, I'm not like them, and it does affect me. Now Maggie wants me to finance her kids' trip to Disneyworld."

"If you're even considering it, you ought to make them earn it," Ty said. "Tell them if they come top of their respective classes for a whole semester you will reward them with the trip."

She sent Ty a beaming smile. "Thanks, I just might. Why didn't I think of that? They'll never do it."

"That's what I figured." Ty briefly touched her hand. "What about your brother?"

"He's the worst of the lot. He blew the fortune Dad gave him trying to run his own bar. Now my ex, who is a chef at Dynasty, has joined forces with him. *"*

Both men seemed impressed. They probably dined there all the time.

"A celebrity chef," Ty said. "Never set foot in the place myself, but there's always write-ups in the papers about it, celebrities behaving badly, stuff like that."

"Jordi was an assistant chef at another joint when we were together. He got headhunted and finished up at Dynasty. *"*

"How long did you date?" Ty asked.

"Two years too long." She wrinkled her nose. "He changed when he finished up at Dynasty. You're right. The celebrity status rubbed off on him, which is when he started criticizing me."

"Chefs in these fancy places get a lot of attention from women. Probably went to his head," Vasco remarked.

"Perhaps. Anyway, I hadn't heard from him for ages, which was fine by me, but now he's back on the scene because he wants something."

"You're dating again?" Ty asked, scowling.

"Hell no, he appeared on my doorstep today to tell me he's decided to open his own restaurant. Pete is going to run the bar and Jordi seems to think he can waltz back into my life and I'll back the scheme financially." She shook her head. "Astonishing. But the worrying thing is that if Jordi and I had stayed together, I would still be the trusting, believing little soul I once was, and most likely *would* have gone along with him."

"People think having money is the cure for all evils," Vasco said softly. "But often it causes more problems than it solves."

"Tell me about it." Sorrel rolled her eyes. "I know I shouldn't let my family make me feel bad, but they know all the right buttons to push and do it pretty damned well."

"They make you feel in the wrong for not supporting their ventures?" Vasco asked.

"Right."

"And they've probably convinced themselves that's the truth," Ty said. "If they resent you so much then I'm guessing it's definitely one of them selling off your ideas."

"You're probably right." Sorrel felt emotionally drained. "I think I've always known that but wasn't ready to face the truth. I talk quite openly about what slogans I'm pitching for in front of them, and they know what channels I go through to get the pitches accepted. They could do it easily enough, but I'm not prepared to accuse any of them without definitive proof."

"Well, that's easily arranged." Vasco said.

"How?"

Vasco signaled for the check. "Come on. It'll be easier to show you."

"Let me get this," she said, reaching for her purse.

"Nope. It's on us."

"Thanks," she said.

"For the meal?" Ty raised a brow. "You only had a salad."

"Thanks for the meal and for not mentioning the death by chocolate." She grinned. "But that's not all I was thanking you for."

"Then what?" Vasco asked, in the process of handing over his credit card.

"For not asking how much I inherited. It's the first thing most people want to know."

"None of our damned business." Vasco stood and helped her from her chair. Marley jumped up at his legs and Vasco laughed, bending to tickle his ears. "This little guy is keen to go."

"We'll follow you back to your place."

Ty took her elbow and helped her down the front steps. She was perfectly capable of managing without his help but it was nice to be in the presence of a gentleman. Besides, the touch of his hand on her arm felt kind of good. Marley pulled them towards the parking lot, straining on the end of his leash. Vasco laughed and took the leash from her, extending his long legs to keep up with the dog's antics. When they reached her car he lifted Marley onto the back seat and waited for her to fasten her seat belt before the two of them headed for a truck parked in the next row.

Sorrel drove back, deep in thought. It had been damned hard to do any in-depth thinking when inundated by so much masculinity and being bombarded with bucket loads of mercurial charm. Her body had sprung enthusiastically to life, like a flower being watered after a long drought. She justified her reaction by reminding herself she would have had to be dead not to react to their animal vitality, or the manner in which they gave her their complete and absolute attention, apparently blind to the many women in the bar keen to attract their attention.

They ran a gym, so she supposed they were used to scantily clad women parading themselves in front of them. They weren't looking upon her as a woman, just a paying client. Presumably they threw in the charisma for free. *Stop being such a cynic.* Whoa, that made her sound like she was paying for sex, and she wasn't quite that desperate yet. Her pussy might feel a little damp right now, her nipples had definitely hardened and were rubbing abrasively against the fabric of her bra as thoughts of having sex with either of them took root in her brain. Sensation was spiraling through her gut, pooling between her legs, no question about that. But that was her guilty secret. They'd laugh themselves silly if they knew. Geez, they must get that reaction all the time.

She held on to the thought that she *did* need their help, and felt better already because they were willing to resolve a problem she was too cowardly to tackle head on.

She wondered why they needed the money she would pay them if they owned a successful gym. Then again, they were acting in their capacity as Raoul's agents. Presumably it was a military thing. She was well aware the military took care of their own.

She quit overanalyzing as she turned onto her street. Things were the way they were. She had set the ball rolling, and would see the thing through to wherever it led, however uncomfortable she was with the outcome. They seemed to think they had a quick fix for her problems. Damn, couldn't they drag it out, just a little? They were pretty sure they would expose a member of her family as the culprit, and she had to agree. Sorrel wasn't sure if she was ready to handle that right now, but knew she had little choice.

She was through with being a doormat. It was time to make a stand.

She pulled into the lot behind her apartment block, indicating to Ty, behind the wheel of their truck, to take one of the visitors' spots. Long jean-clad legs spilled from both sides of the truck and they ambled over to join her.

"Which is yours?" Vasco asked.

"That one," she replied, pointing to a first floor unit with its own small yard.

"Hmm, easy enough to get in, being on the first floor."

Marley ran ahead as Sorrel fished her keys from her purse and opened the front door. She had switched her phone back on while in the car, and it had already rung twice, her brother and then Jordi. She ignored them both.

"Come on in," she said, sighing when it rang for a third time. Pete again.

Vasco and Ty paused on the threshold to examine the lock.

"No sign of forced entry," Ty said.

Sorrel wondered how they could know that. Marley ran into the main room, with its open kitchen to one side, and jumped up onto his favorite chair. The guys examined the space and Sorrel felt nervous as she watched their gazes roving slowly over everything, computing it all. She knew this apartment wasn't anything much, and she could afford much better now. But she had lived here a long time and hadn't even thought about upgrading. She had made it comfortable and homely. There was more than enough space for her, it was in a convenient part of town, and it was easy to keep clean. The furniture was good quality, but minimal, with bright throw cushions scattered about, scented candles ready to light when darkness fell, shelves full of books, and some decent pictures on the wall.

"Nice," Vasco said, probably just to be…well, nice.

"Thanks."

"Is this where you work?" Ty asked, pointing to the table in the breakfast nook, which housed her computer and a load of office supplies.

"Very astute of you," she replied grinning.

"Hmm."

Ty took a weird implement like a wand from the bag he'd carried in from his truck and waved it about.

"What's he doing?" she asked Vasco.

"Checking for listening devices," Vasco replied calmly, like it was the most natural thing in the world.

"You have got to be kidding me!"

"You'd be surprised what we find. I know it sounds high-tech, but nowadays you can buy just about anything online. And people do. Trust me on this."

"It's clean," Ty said, putting away his magic wand.

"Good to know," Sorrel said, now feeling a little uncomfortable.

"Hey, don't freak out on me, babe." Vasco placed a large warm hand on her back, then thought better of it and threw his entire arm around both shoulders. "We have to assume whoever's stealing your ideas has either visual or audible access to your space."

"Not a comforting thought."

But leaning against the solid wall of warmth and safety that passed for Vasco's chest was a little *too* comforting. He hadn't removed his arm so she felt justified in snuggling, just for a moment or two. After all, it wasn't every day a girl got to hear someone might have bugged her living space. *Yeah, right. That's the only reason you need to cuddle.*

"We've ruled out audible, so my guess is that someone comes in here when you're out and about," Ty said. "Are you a creature of habit, darlin'?"

Darlin'? "Well, yes, I suppose so. Especially since I got Marley. He and I go to the park first thing, every day."

"Well then, that probably explains it."

Ty put his bag down, rummaged about in it and produced a very small item. He then looked around Sorrel's work space, concentrating on the area directly above it. There was a ventilation grill at the juncture with the ceiling, which Ty appeared to find fascinating.

"That ought to do it."

With Vasco's arm still around her shoulders, she watched as Ty climbed on a chair and removed the grill from the front of the vent with a screwdriver. He fitted the thingy he had taken from his bag into the vent, fiddled around, making adjustments for a while, then replaced the grill.

"All done," he said, jumping off the chair and returning it to the table.

"I don't suppose you want to tell me—"

"It's a digital camera activated by movement," Vasco explained. "If you work on the breakfast bar for now it will save you being on candid camera."

"Oh, okay," she said weakly.

"The important thing to remember is, when you go out, leave all your papers where you normally would," Ty said.

"Leave slogans you have no intention of using in clear view, but keep all the good stuff on you at all times. Can you do that?" Vasco asked.

"Sure. How long do the batteries last in the camera? How long before we catch the guy?"

"A few days to the first question," Ty said. "No idea to the second."

"But here's the deal," Vasco added. "Wear something pretty tomorrow evening. We'll pick you up around seven and check the camera at the same time."

"Where are we going?" she asked, a combination of bewilderment and excitement gripping her when it occurred to her they were not abandoning her quite yet.

"You'll see," Vasco replied, twitching her nose. "But in the meantime, don't feel frightened. No one's out to hurt you. They only want to steal your ideas."

"If we thought you were in danger, we wouldn't leave you alone," Ty said, serious for once.

"I've never felt physically threatened," she assured them.

"That's good," Ty said, winking at her.

"You must let me pay you a retainer," she said. "All this dashing back and forth from Port Angeles when you have a business to run must eat into your time and profits."

"We'll talk about that when the job's done."

To her astonishment, Vasco dropped a light kiss on her lips as he removed the arm from around her shoulders. "Will you be okay?" he asked.

"Yeah, sure," she replied.

Ty moved in and kissed her as well, also on the lips. "Don't worry, darlin'," he said. "We'll get the creep who's not playing fair." He put on a silly voice that made her smile. "We always get our man."

"Or woman," Vasco added.

Sorrel just bet they did.

Chapter Five

"You guys look hot." Jenner, the gym's manager who'd broken the hearts of half the single men in Port Angeles by coming out, looked up from behind the reception desk. "Got dates?"

It was five the following afternoon and the guys had just come down from the apartment they shared on the top floor of their business premises. Jenner usually only ever saw them in workout gear or jeans. Tonight both were wearing sharp pants and fashionably long dress shirts worn outside the waistbands.

"I was going to ask the same question." Lauren came up behind them and placed a hand proprietorially on Vasco's arm. "Not sure I'm woman enough for the both of you, but I'll sure as hell give it my best shot."

"There are worse ways to die," Jenner said, sending the guys a mischievous grin. Vasco replied with a look that warned her he'd get his revenge later. Not that he ever would, and they both knew it. Jenner was a godsend. Good at her job, better with the clients, especially the difficult ones, and willing to work for way less than she was worth. Better yet, her sexual orientation ensured she didn't hit on them, so they could enjoy a profitable business relationship that had become a friendship.

Put simply, *Body Language* couldn't function without Jenner and Vasco and Ty both knew it.

"We're checking out a new client," Vasco said, which was kinda true. "I'm surprised to see you here in the evening, Lauren. I thought you were done for the day. Can't keep away, huh?"

"I figured I'd give Cassie's spinning class a whirl," she said.

"Well, that's good. But remember, too much exercise is almost as bad as too little." Vasco turned back to Jenner. "Call us if you have problems."

"I've got it covered, boys," Jenner said. "Have fun. It's about time you got out of here for a while."

"Enjoy the spinning, Lauren," Vasco called over his shoulder.

"Wonder who the lucky ladies are," they heard Lauren mutter petulantly to Jenner.

"Phew," Vasco said as they strode towards their truck. "That was a close call."

"You think Lauren didn't have her mind just on spinning?" Ty pulled a shocked face, but spoiled the effect by grinning. "You astound me."

"She was here to get her claws into one of us, no question. Did you see her face when we said we'd be back late?" Vasco opened the truck and turned the key in the ignition. "I really can't afford to upset her, but there are limits to the sacrifices I'm prepared to make for the sake of our bank balance. But if you—"

"Fuck, no!"

Vasco laughed as he pulled onto the highway. "That's what I figured."

"Now, ask me the same question about the lady we're about to see and I might just be willing to oblige."

Vasco pulled a wry face. "Don't put yourself out."

"I hate that she has such little self-esteem." Ty kicked moodily at the crooked mat in the foot-well of the truck. "Her family have really worked a number on her."

"Well, we do have plans to fix that, remember. We owe it to her as part of the service to make her feel better about herself."

Ty shook his head. "I wish we could do a thorough job, but she ain't a player."

"She could be."

"I know, but I don't wanna hurt her. She would be a keeper, and I don't think either of us want that right now."

"We can't afford the distraction if we're gonna get ourselves out from under the pile of debt we've accrued." Vasco flipped the indicator and moved past a slow Lincoln loaded with seniors. "Let's just see our plan through this evening, and then play it by ear."

"Gotcha."

They reached Sorrel's apartment half an hour early. Assuming she wouldn't be ready, they were prepared to check the camera feed while she got her act together. They were surprised when she opened the door to them, looking good enough to devour instead of the fancy meal they had planned for her. Vasco had suspected the ubiquitous little black dress would be the order of the night. All women tended to hide behind black when they didn't like their bodies.

All except Sorrel, it seemed.

She wore a cerise sheath with a high neckline that clung to her tits but didn't reveal an inch of cleavage. It skimmed over her wide middle and finished at her knee. She had bulky thighs, as Vasco knew from having briefly touched one, but very shapely lower legs. They were showcased tonight in thin black stockings, and neat black shoes with four-inch heels adorned her small feet. Her hair was loose and freshly washed, cascading around her shoulders in a riot of unruly curls. She wore minimum makeup and smelled of a light, floral fragrance that suited her personality and tested Vasco's resolve to keep his hands to himself.

He and Ty simply stood there and gaped at her. Sorrel obviously misinterpreted their reaction and blushed.

"You said to dress up," she told them defensively. "Is this too much?"

"It's goddamned perfect," Vasco replied, leaning in to kiss her.

"What he said," Ty added, taking his turn to steal a kiss.

"Well then, thank you. Come on in. Can I get you something to drink?"

Their response was delayed while they dealt with Marley who, presumably associating Vasco's voice with illicit steak, hurled himself at them both in a frenzy of wagging delight. They laughed as they petted him and the mutt rolled on his back, offering up his belly for a good scratch. Vasco found a ball up against the baseboard and rolled it across the room, sending the dog scrabbling off in pursuit of it.

"He'll keep you at that all night," Sorrel said, laughing.

They declined her offer of drinks, but Ty checked his camera.

"Nothing," he said, replacing the grill. "You didn't get any uninvited guests today."

"Good. I'm used to my own company, but I still felt a bit awkward last night and found it hard to sleep, knowing my space has been invaded. It made me so damned mad." She grinned. "I took a baseball bat to bed with me. If anyone had broken in, I would have used it, no question."

"I'm glad you didn't have to." Vasco smiled at her. "Are you ready?"

She picked up her purse. Marley reached the door first, wagging because he thought he was coming too.

"Not tonight, buddy," Ty said. "But we promise you a walk in the park later. Deal?"

Ty offered his hand and the mutt raised a paw, making Vasco laugh because he seemed to know how to shake.

"Did you teach him to do that?" he asked Sorrel.

"No, he figured it out all by himself." She shook her head. "Precocious doesn't come close to describing Marley, but he's too adorable for it to be a problem."

She picked up her cell phone, about to put it in her purse. Vasco plucked it from her grasp.

"You won't be needing that tonight."

"But what about…what if…work, you know?"

"Do you get work calls at night?"

"Well, no."

"Clients will leave a message if they need to talk to you, so you won't lose any business. But your family will bug you if you take the phone with you."

"I don't need to take their calls."

"No," Vasco said, sending her an enticing grin that heated the air between them. "But you will because it's what you're programed to do. You can't help yourself."

"True, but—"

"How many times have you heard from them since yesterday?" Ty asked.

"Okay, point taken. The phone stays." She shared a smile between them. "It's kinda liberating, actually."

"Attagirl!" Vasco replied. "Got anything to occupy Marley to compensate for leaving him?"

"It's so sweet of you to think of him."

"Aw, honey, don't call him sweet." Ty pulled an agonized face. "I'm the sweet one. He's just plain mean."

She laughed as she rummaged in a kitchen cabinet, came up with a rawhide bone that was almost as big as the little dog, and threw it to him. Marley managed to get his jaws around it, barely, and settled down with the bone perched on his front paws, already gnawing away at it.

"I happen to know you're both real nice guys, but I promise not to let on. Your secret's safe with me."

"Phew." Ty wiped imaginary sweat from his brow. "I thought for a minute we'd been busted."

He opened the front door, took Sorrel's keys from her and turned the deadbolt.

"Are you going to tell me where we're going?" Sorrel asked as Vasco helped her slide onto the front seat of the truck. Ty climbed in on her opposite side. It felt good, naturally right, to have her there between them, but Vasco pushed the thought aside. Now wasn't the time.

"What, and spoil the surprise?"

They pulled up a short time later in front of Dynasty. Vasco helped Sorrel from the truck and handed the keys to the valet. She appeared preoccupied and it took her a moment to realize where they were.

"This is where Jordi works," she said, looking panicked and a little disappointed at their lack of sensitivity. "We can't go in there."

"It's because Jordi works here that we made a reservation," Ty replied.

He took one of her elbows, Vasco took the other, and they walked her beneath the awning into the restaurant itself, not giving her time to voice further objections. The hostess was upon them in seconds, her face wreathed in smiles that excluded Sorrel.

"She's checking out your butts," Sorrel muttered, sounding amused.

"We work hard on our butts," Ty replied, winking at her. "They're worth checking out. Wanna have a go?"

"Don't be shy," she responded, blushing. God, but she was adorable when she blushed. Vasco couldn't remember the last time he'd interacted with a female who blushed so readily. He liked her comparative innocence, even though the thoughts that occupied his mind, the things he'd like to do to her, were far from innocent. "Say what's on your mind."

"Your table's ready. Please follow me."

The hostess picked up three menus and sashayed ahead of them, swinging her hips in a provocative invitation for the guys to return the favor and check out her ass.

"Don't ever walk like that," Vasco said in an undertone to Sorrel.

"Like I could. I don't exactly have the hips for it. Or the ass."

"Thank fuck for that."

She blinked up at him, clearly confused. He would explain later. Perhaps. In the meantime, his cryptic comment had taken her mind off where they were. Vasco glanced across at Ty as they were shown to a booth and Sorrel slid into the middle of the horseshoe-shaped seat, leaving the guys to take up the places on either side of her.

"Would you mind telling me what we're doing here?" she demanded, as soon as the hostess left them.

"I want to see your ex in action," Vasco said.

"You should have warned me."

"Would you have agreed to come if we had?" Ty asked.

"Thought not," Vasco said when she looked away without answering. "Just trust us to know what we're doing, and play along. Okay?"

"I guess."

They looked at the menu and Vasco tried not to wince at the prices. They could probably get away with it as a business expense, but right now he didn't give a fuck if they couldn't. He couldn't remember the last time he and Ty had taken a whole evening off from the business and relaxed in the company of a woman they both liked, and who needed their help. It felt good to be needed.

"Anything take your fancy?" he asked Sorrel.

"Lots of things, but you have to let me deal with the check."

"Nope. Our treat," Ty replied promptly.

"That's not fair. You're only here to help me."

"Helping ladies in distress is what we do best," Vasco said, briefly placing a hand on her thigh. "Now quit arguing with us." He lowered his voice to a seductive purr. "When you get to know us a little better, you'll realize we're always in charge and arguing with us has consequences."

She rolled her eyes. "I don't need to know you better. I already got that part."

"I doubt it," Ty said. "But that could all change."

Vasco shot his buddy a warning look. "Right, here's our server. Have you decided what you'd like to eat, babe?"

Vasco wondered how long it would be before the mighty chef noticed Sorrel's presence. He strolled into the restaurant in full chef regalia when they were halfway through their entrees, stopping at tables to accept the acclamations he seemed to think were his due. His food *was* good, Vasco conceded. So it fucking should be at these prices.

"Good evening," he said, stepping up to their table. "I do hope everything is…Sorrel, what the fu—"

"Hey, Jordi," she said, smiling up at the jerk with every appearance of outward calm that Vasco gave her top marks for. He knew she was anything but calm and again placed a reassuring hand on her thigh. "Excellent food."

Jordi's gaze darted between Vasco and Ty, his eyes narrowing with suspicion. Vasco tried to remain neutral and give him the benefit of the doubt, but had already decided he hated the man. "You should have warned me you were coming. I would have made sure you got a better table."

"This one's just great, thanks."

"Who are your friends?"

"We're business associates of Sorrel's," Vasco replied easily.

"Business, but you…I mean." He glowered at Sorrel. "We need to talk."

"We are talking, Jordi."

"I mean properly."

"We're kinda busy right now," Ty said. "And our food's getting cold. You'll have to excuse us."

Sorrel let out a nervous giggle when Jordi strode away, his back rigid with disapproval. "I wouldn't want to be in his kitchen right now," she said. "I know what he's like when he gets mad. Someone's in for it." She turned toward Vasco. "Why did you tell him we were business partners?"

"Well, it's not exactly a lie."

She sighed. "I wish you'd tell me what you two are up to. I think I've handled things pretty well up until now. Don't treat me like a child. I'm a big girl and don't need protecting."

"You have handled things superbly," Ty agreed. Vasco noticed his buddy's hand seeking out Sorrel's other thigh. Sorrel was either too preoccupied to notice, or she didn't mind them feeling her up. "We asked you to leave your cell behind because we figured the moment Jordi saw you with us, he would feel threatened and call your brother. Your brother will try to call you, but—"

"But can't reach me." She nodded. "That's clever, but I don't see what it has to do with my stolen slogans."

"It has to do with you not being ripped off by your family," Vasco said, more forcefully than he'd intended. "We want to help you stand up to them. You won't get any peace until you do." He cut her a seriously intent grin—one that had always gotten him his way in the past. "No extra charge."

"Ten bucks says your brother will appear here within half an hour," Ty said, leaning back on the banquette, still with his hand massaging Sorrel's thigh.

Ty was wrong. Pete burst through the doors just twenty minutes later and homed in on their table.

"Not exactly subtle, is he?" Vasco remarked. "I assume that's your brother."

"That's him," she responded, pinching the bridge of her nose as though she had a headache threatening.

"Hey, Sorrel," Pete said, standing in front of their table. "Jordi rang me to say you were here."

"No shit."

"Sorrel, since when did you start swearing?"

"Oh, give me a break, Pete. I am an adult, in case it escaped your notice."

"What are you doing here?"

"Er, eating dinner."

"Who are these guys?"

"Where are your manners?" Sorrel shot back. "These are my friends, this is a private dinner and you're intruding."

"You didn't mention you were planning on coming here."

She raised one brow in an arrogantly disdainful gesture. "Any reason why I should?"

"I could have joined you."

"You could have invited me here yourself, seeing as how you appear to be so at home with Jordi."

Vasco wanted to applaud. She was getting mad, holding her own like she probably wouldn't have if she'd known what they had planned for her. He figured it felt good. His mind flashed back to a previous life and he *knew* it did.

"I've lost my appetite," Vasco said. "Shall we skip dessert, babe, and carry on our discussion somewhere more private?"

"Fine by me."

"I'll call you later, make sure you got home okay," Pete said before walking away.

Vasco caught their server's attention. "Check, please," he said.

"That's the best fun I've had in years," Sorrel said, linking an arm through each of theirs as they left the restaurant, conscious of Pete and Jordi's death glares boring into their backs. "Thank you."

"Our pleasure," Ty assured her.

"You okay?" Vasco asked. "You're kinda quiet."

Sorrel threw her head back and closed her eyes. "How did you know they'd do that?"

"What, come and check us out?" Ty grinned. "Educated guess."

"Hmm."

She said nothing more and they drove the short distance back to Sorrel's apartment in silence. When they got there, Marley greeted them as though he'd been deserted for days. Ty tugged his ears and volunteered to take him around the block.

"Thanks," Sorrel said. "I'll make us some coffee. You'll need a caffeine hit, I expect, before the drive back."

Ty clipped on Marley's leash and slipped out the door.

"About that," Vasco said, leaning against the kitchen surface, watching as she ground beans for the coffee. "We were thinking a little vacation would work for you."

"Come again?"

Oh baby, if only! "Your family is gonna hound you night and day, now that they've seen us together and think we're after your money, just like they are."

"I handled them okay tonight. Well, I handled Pete, anyway. I don't see why they should drive me from my home." She filled the kettle and flipped it on. "Anyway, where were you planning on sending me?"

"Back to *Body Language,* with us."

"What!" She turned to face him, looking truly horrified. "You want me to go to a gym?" Her face crumpled. "Do I look as bad as all that?"

Chapter Six

Sorrel, at first horrified when she realized where they were to dine, had actually enjoyed kicking ass. Seeing Jordi and then Pete slack-jawed with shock had made her feel empowered. Of course, Vasco and Ty made that possible. They had her back—or rather, her thighs—and gave her the courage to tell her brother and ex to take a hike.

Damn, it had felt good!

She'd enjoyed dining with two such head-turning hunks even more. They ignored all the speculative glances and not so subtle come-ons they got from various women in the restaurant, including the hostess. Sorrel was sure she saw her try to slip her phone number to Vasco. But Vasco and Ty only had eyes for her, which was nothing short of miraculous. She relaxed in their company, reveling in the admiration she thought she saw in their eyes, starting with when she opened the door to them in her cerise dress. She'd bought it new that day with dinner in mind, blinking at the astronomical cost of it, even though she could well afford it. It would be a long time before Sorrel remembered she didn't have to count every cent anymore.

But now Vasco was not so subtly reminding her that she needed to drop a few pounds. Well, more than a few—like she wasn't well aware. They were no different than anyone else after all, and had only been trying to make her feel good about herself because she'd hired them to do a job. But not *that* job. She had known all along they were just being kind, of course she had, but still…

"Aw, honey, there is absolutely nothing wrong with the way you look."

"Save it, Vasco," she said, turning her back on him and fiddling with the coffee-maker. "And thanks for the offer, but no thanks. If I ever decide to go to a gym, there are plenty to choose from in Seattle. Your job is done. Show me how to use that camera, I'll discover who's stealing from me, and deal with it myself. Send me your bill and I'll settle up by return."

His hands landed on her shoulders, sending warmth searing through the fabric of her dress directly into her skin, replacing her hurt and anger with shock. She felt his large body pressing against her back, hot and hard, causing her breath to hitch and making her wonder what it was he wanted from her.

"We invited you to *Body Language* because it's where we live, and because you need a break from your family, is all. You don't need to step foot in the gym."

"You live over the shop?" She hadn't stopped to consider their living arrangements.

"Yeah."

Her body appeared to have relaxed into his without her permission. God, it felt good to lean against that rock-hard physique. A girl could get used to it—but not this girl. She quickly pulled away again, aware she couldn't afford to let her guard down with a calculating sophisticate who could so easily steal her heart. She had his measure now. He definitely wanted something from her, just like everyone else in her life appeared to. He was just more subtle in the way he went about it, to say nothing of his persuasive methods, which certainly bucked the regular trend.

He wrapped one strong arm around her waist and forced her to lean back again whether she wanted to or not. Oh, she wanted to! Sorrel couldn't remember the last time she had wanted something more, but she was damned if she would wilt beneath his skilful hands, as she was sure just about every female he laid them on tended to.

"What do you want from me?" she asked in a stricken tone, horrified when tears welled and threatened to fall. "Why not just come right out and say it? It would save a lot of time that way."

"Oh, baby!"

He turned her in his arms and she fought against him every step of the way, knowing it would be dangerous to look into his face. But he was too strong for her puny efforts to make any difference and before she knew it her tits were squashed against his granite chest as one large finger gently trapped a tear as it slid down her cheek.

"You don't have any idea, do you?" he asked softly, his breath peppering her face as she looked up at him with a combination of anguish and uncertainty.

"About what?"

"About how much you have going for you. About how sensational you looked tonight. About how damned stoked Ty and I were to be seen with you."

"You...seen with me." She shook her head, wondering what they must be on. "I don't think—"

"You think too much, that's your problem." He ran the pad of his thumb across her lips, sending a glorious shudder ricocheting through her. "You think about everything and everyone except yourself."

"There's nothing to think about."

"I disagree. Every head in that restaurant turned to look at you tonight when you walked through. I was so damned jealous—"

"Me!" She widened her eyes. "You've got that all wrong. They were looking at you and Ty."

"The women might have been, but didn't you see the men checking you out?"

"They were not!"

But now that she came to think about it, she *had* seen a few male heads turn her way.

"Yeah, that's right." Vasco looked impossibly smug. "Now you're getting it."

"They were looking to see what their women were looking at."

Vasco shook his head, his expression exasperated. "What am I going to do with you, darlin'?"

"I know you're only trying to make me feel better, and I appreciate it, really I do, but I know what I look like."

"Is that right?"

His voice was so smooth, so sexy and provocative, that it wrapped itself around her like a comfort blanket—reassuring, addictive.

"Hmm," she murmured.

Damn it, what was his question? She was sure there had been one, but it was so hard to think with her body pressed against his, his lips so temptingly close. Her monosyllabic responses probably made him think she was moronic as well as fat.

"Not being a stick insect isn't necessarily a bad thing."

She harrumphed. "Tell that to the fashion magazines."

"Don't read 'em."

"I don't, but it's hard to escape the fact that the world thinks skinny is best. It's everywhere you look."

"Ask any man for his opinion. Ask all those men who checked you out in the restaurant tonight." He paused, tightening the arm that held her captive against his body as though he thought she might try and make a break for it. *As if!* "Ask Ty and me. I think you'll find all men prefer a woman with a few curves."

"A few, and in the right places."

"See, you're doing it again." He wagged a finger at her. "Keep contradicting me and you'll earn yourself a spanking."

Holy moly, was he serious about that? She glanced up at him and his taunting sure as hell made him look it. She'd heard about men like him, but never thought to meet one. Better not to ask him what he meant. She could tell he wanted her to, and Sorrel never was good at doing the right thing.

"You probably haven't noticed the size of my ass," she said, some death wish making her determined to draw her imperfections to his attention.

He chuckled. "Darlin', women are getting buttock implants nowadays."

"Yeah, and I've never been able to understand that." She frowned. "Why would anyone *choose* to have a butt that looks like a shelf?"

Vasco shrugged. "You've got me there. I guess we all want what we haven't got. I see it every day at the gym."

"If it's true what you say about me, why haven't the men been beating a path to my door?"

"You were dating the jerk, up until the time your dad passed. I don't have you pegged as the type who would cheat."

"No, I've always been loyal."

"Then, I'm guessing here, you turned yourself into a bit of a recluse after that, so you could grieve in private. But I figure you were asked on lots of dates before you and Jordi got hot and heavy."

"Well, yes, I suppose, but—"

"I rest my case," he said smugly.

"Oh, for goodness sake!" She thumped his chest. It was like hitting a brick wall, and he didn't even seem to feel it. "You are impossibly arrogant."

"I get that a lot." He sent her a wicked smile, the significance of which failed to hit home until it was too late for her to take evasive action. *Yeah, like that was gonna happen.* "But right now you are in dire need of a kiss."

He lowered his head to close the distance between them and slanted his lips over hers with an assurance that made it obvious he didn't expect any objections. A devilish part of Sorrel wanted to reject him, just to put him in his place. The moment his lips firmed against hers, she forgot all about objecting, and kissed him right back. Her arms slid around his neck, playing with the hair at his nape, pressing her tits more firmly against his chest because however close she got to him, it didn't seem close enough. He drew on her lower lip, clearly wanting her to open for him. Again, thoughts of playing hard to get filtered through her muzzy brain, but evaporated as soon as his tongue slid past her guard and cut a path through her mouth, velvety and sensuous, promising so much.

She blamed his damned hands for distracting her, for sending spirals of desire shooting through her in dizzying waves that made coherent thought next to impossible. The hands in question had somehow splayed themselves against her ass, as though to prove a point following on from their recent discussion. He massaged the embarrassingly large globes, pressing her more tightly against an impressive erection. The fact that she could arouse him to such heights gave her confidence a timely boost. Then again, an erection was an erection. If he was well-endowed—and he obviously was— then of course it would be of eye-watering proportions. Pity she'd never get better acquainted with it.

Vasco's tongue maneuvered with limber skill as the kiss became unashamedly carnal. Geez, this guy knew how to turn on a girl's lights! Vasco was right. Sometimes she thought too much. She emptied her mind and concentrated upon returning his kiss, her pulse skittering in her veins as her body coursed with readiness and her turbulent emotions went off the scale. She couldn't remember the last time she had felt so aroused, or if she ever had. She really needed to get laid, and this time her vibrator probably wouldn't be up to the job.

She tried to suppress a little squeal of protest when he broke the kiss, but it slipped out anyway. Vasco chuckled and ran a finger gently down the curve of her face.

"I guess we both needed that," he said.

"Hardly professional behavior, Mr. Blaine," she replied, trying to treat the incident as casually as he obviously could, but ruining the effect by sounding breathless and probably having a flushed face. He, on the other hand, looked totally cool. Insufferable man!

"I'm off the clock."

"Ah, that makes it all right then."

She wriggled free of his arms, and this time he let her go. She moved slightly out of range, aware she would never be able to formulate a coherent sentence if he touched her again. Her body was still on fire, her mind in turmoil, her pussy throbbing with need. Damn, she was a mess, and no longer knew what to think about his interest in her. What she did know was that it would be impossible to fake the type of passion he put into that kiss. Well, impossible for her, but he probably did that sort of thing all the time.

"What's going on, Vasco?" she asked, leaning against the counter, coffee forgotten, arms folded beneath her breasts.

"Okay, here's the thing. I figured your ex would see us in his restaurant, and wondered if he'd call your brother. He did, which implies a financial interest in you." His slow, sexy smile caused her pussy to leak and her annoyance at his arbitrary actions to fade away. "I didn't like the jerk, but I rather hoped he wouldn't call Pete, meaning his interest in you was personal."

"So, we've established they want to rip me off, but I already knew that."

"So do your mother and sister." He fixed her with a smoldering look. "And I don't mean to put you down, babe, but if you stay here where they can get at you, how long will it be before one or the other of them wears you down? As you said yourself, they know all the right buttons to push."

"And you think that by showing up with you guys, it will make them think I have immoral support?"

"Good choice of words." He grinned at her. "They know now you're not the pushover they were hoping you were."

"Thank you for that, but I still don't see why I need to come back to your place."

His eyes shimmered with hot intentions. "Oh, I can think of several pressing reasons."

"Vasco!"

"Sorry," he replied, not looking the least bit repentant. "But you did ask. And seriously, you *do* need a break, and to have some fun. To put yourself first for a change. Besides, if they can't get to you, they'll wonder where you are *and* the slogan thief will almost certainly strike while you're away. We'll pop back at the weekend and check the camera then."

"Why are you going to so much trouble on my account?"

"Why?" He seemed surprised by the question. "Why would we not? You need help and we're in a position to provide it for you."

"Hmm." She thought there was more to it than that. She had noticed a shadow pass through Vasco's eyes whenever her grasping family was mentioned and wondered if this was personal for him.

"So, will you come?" He tilted his head and sent her a puerile smile that melted her insides. Why was she even hesitating? What was the worst that could happen? Most women in her position would grasp the opportunity, and any body parts up for grabs, with both hands. "We can be real good fun. I promise."

She just bet they could. "I suppose, if you put it like that. I don't have much work at the moment, and what I do have I can take with me. Perhaps a change of scene will inspire me to wax lyrical about toilet cleaner."

"Come again?"

She smiled. "Never mind. You really don't want to know. I'll throw a few things in a bag." She walked toward the doorway, then paused as a thought occurred to her. "Oh, what about Marley?"

"He's invited, too, obviously."

"Okay, but one more thing. I won't need to wear Lycra, will I?" She shuddered. "I should hate to give your gym a bad name."

Vasco roared with laughter. "Baby, you see some of the sights we see every day, and you'll stop worrying. Besides, I already told you, you don't need to step foot in the gym, unless you want to."

"Can't see that happening. Exercise and I aren't comfortable bedfellows."

"Oh yeah." His face lit up with an enticingly heated grin and she knew she'd said the wrong thing. "So what does make you comfortable in bed?"

"Hot cocoa and a good book."

She heard his throaty chuckle, and thought he muttered something about that being a crying shame, as she ran to her bedroom. Flirting with an expert, which she realized with a jolt was what she had been doing, was exhausting. It was also a game she'd never win. She pulled a bag from her closet and started throwing clothes into it before she lost her nerve. Now she was out of reach of Vasco's marauding hands, she could think a little more rationally, but not to the extent that she could figure out why the guys were insisting she went back with them. They were going above and beyond…way beyond.

"Just go with the flow," she said aloud, wondering what clothes to take with her. Casual, she figured. Well, apart from her new dress, she didn't have much else. She grabbed a few toiletries from her bathroom, zipped up the bag, and was as ready as she would ever be. She heard the front door open and the next moment Marley launched himself onto the bed. She absently stroked his ears, aware of the guys talking in muted tones in the other room. She moved closer to the door and heard Ty give a little whoop when Vasco told him she'd agreed to go with them. Like there was any serious doubt about that. Why was Ty so pleased, though?

Bottom line, she liked the guys, but didn't altogether trust them. But, for once, she would live for the moment and see what shook loose. They had made her feel special tonight, and for that alone she owed them. She wondered if she ought to change out of her dress. Probably not suitable for where she was going. They she recalled how impressed the guys seemed by it, how good it felt to be admired, and defiantly left it on.

"All set," she said, wandering back into the main room.

Vasco grabbed the bag from her hand. "I've got that," he said.

"And I've got Marley's bed and toys," Ty added, winking at her. "So glad you agreed to come, babe."

"Vasco was very persuasive."

Ty chuckled. "I'll just bet he was."

"Don't forget your laptop and any papers you might need. And to leave something to interest your intruder."

Sorrel would have forgotten, for which she held the pair of them entirely responsible. Having them in her space was overwhelming. They were so big, so masculine, so drop-dead gorgeous that she kept thinking she was imagining things. But no, they were there, large as life and twice as dangerous.

And she was going to be their houseguest. Surreal!

"Right, then, that looks like everything," Vasco said. "Let's go."

She found herself carrying nothing but her purse as the guys took everything else from her, including Marley, who appeared enamored of them. They waited with her, protective as she locked the front door, then threw her things onto the back seat of the truck and helped her into the front. Marley jumped onto her lap, Ty slid behind the wheel, and Vasco got in on her opposite side.

"Right," Ty said cheerfully as he fired up the engine. "Let's get this show on the road."

Sure, Sorrel thought, still a little overwhelmed, but what show precisely was he referring to?

Chapter Seven

Traffic was light and Ty made the eighty-mile trip in just over an hour. None of them spoke much, but the radio, tuned to a country station, cut through any tension there might otherwise have been. Tension created by Sorrel, who clearly couldn't decide if she'd done the right thing. Hardly surprising, Ty thought, given she'd only known him and Vasco for five minutes. They could be ax murderers, white slavers or, like the rest of her family, fortune hunters. He could easily imagine such thoughts filtering through her brain, and hoped they could put her at her ease. Damn it, she had so much going for her, but any self-confidence she might have possessed had been whittled away, simply because she didn't like the way she looked.

Ty hoped like heck they could persuade her to play with them, even though he shouldn't be thinking that way. She was a client, the daughter of a military colleague, and it would be taking advantage of her vulnerability, her dependence upon them, her desperation for approval. Even so, his mind wouldn't stop veering in that direction. He knew without having to ask that Vasco was thinking the same way. She was special, no question—the more so because she didn't know it.

"We're just entering Port Angeles now," Ty told her, his voice breaking through the deep silence and the dog's snores. The little guy was curled up in Sorrel's lap, dead to the world. "Our city proudly boasts the largest prehistoric Indian village and burial ground found in the States." Shit, he sounded like a tour guide. "Still, I guess you must already know that, being born and raised in Seattle."

"I haven't been out this way for a while," she said, yawning. "But I do remember some pretty countryside."

"Oh yeah." It was Vasco who answered her. "Majestic Olympic mountains, rain forests, pristine wilderness coastline. Nature of steroids. We got it all."

"You're not city dwellers?"

"We can do cities, if we need to," Ty said, "but we like open spaces and fresh air better."

"My dad was like that," she said. "He didn't used to be, but the military changed him and he started to feel claustrophobic in the city. I guess the things he saw, and stuff…"

"Yeah, we can relate to that." Ty swung the truck into the lot behind the gym, situated several blocks back from the famous pier in an industrial part of town that didn't make the tourist guides. "Right, here we are. Home sweet home."

He and Vasco grabbed her stuff from the rear seat while Marley roamed the lot, lifting his leg frequently, getting acquainted with his surroundings. Sorrel stared up at the outside of the building, which probably didn't inspire confidence, and almost certainly wasn't what she expected. Hopefully it wouldn't cause her to have second or third thoughts about her decision to join them.

"It's not the best part of town," Vasco said, walking up behind her and placing a hand on her shoulder. "But it's safe."

"I wasn't judging. It's just not what I expected."

"It's a converted warehouse," Ty told her as Vasco ran his electronic card through the reader and the door beeped open.

"Doesn't that mean anyone with a membership card can get in any time?" she asked, presumably picking up on Vasco's remark about safety.

"No, we close at ten at night, in about fifteen minutes to be precise. Once we lock the doors, the alarm goes on and the security system won't let anyone without a master key in or out."

"Oh, I see." But she still seemed dubious, especially when a guy with bulging biceps and a menacing expression crashed through the door, nodded to them and jumped into a car. "I guess that's all right then."

"We've got you, babe," Vasco said softly.

"I know, and I guess this place is safer than my apartment, given that someone appears to be in and out of it at will."

"Not for much longer," Ty said, scowling.

They stepped into the open-plan gym, with the pipework exposed on the ceilings from when it used to be a grain store. Now it was all expensive wooden floors, lots of mirrors, and even more expensive equipment. She looked around with apparent interest, but seemed a little overawed. If she really never had been in a gym before, it would be a lot to take in. One or two late-night gym rats were hard at work, sweating away with loose weights and on some of the machines.

"Impressive," she said. "Although I don't have anything to compare it to. I am absolutely not going to ask what some of those instruments of torture are supposed to do to a body."

Vasco laughed. "Probably best not to," he said.

"Did you guys set this operation up from scratch?"

"Yep," Vasco replied, scooping Marley up before he got squashed by a treadmill he seemed fascinated by. "We had to sell our souls to the city to get the necessary permits, but it's working out."

Jenner came up to them, looking trim and very pretty in tight-fitting Lycra. Ty noticed Sorrel's face fall.

"Hey, Jenner," Vasco said. "Any problems?"

"No, we've been quite busy, though."

"That's good," Ty replied. "Say, this is Sorrel. She's staying here with us for a while." Jenner's brows elevated fractionally, presumably because he and Vasco never invited anyone to share their personal space. "Sorrel, this is Jenner, the manager of the gym and our right-hand person. This place would fall apart without her."

"Ah, so this would be a good time to ask for a raise then?"

"Sorry." Vasco placed a hand to his ear. "It's kinda loud in here. Did someone say something?"

Ty laughed along with everyone else, but knew Jenner had a point. They paid her as much as they could afford, which was way less than she was worth, and way more than they paid themselves. She had personal reasons for staying with them, when she could do way better elsewhere. They had promised to pay her more just as soon as they turned a profit, and kept Jenner appraised of their financial situation every step of the way. So far she had remained completely loyal and showed no signs of jumping a ship that was barely remaining afloat. If that day ever came, God alone knew how they would replace her.

"Oh well, it was worth a try." Smiling, Jenner extended a hand. "Nice to meet you, Sorrel. Welcome to the mad house."

"Nice meeting you, too," she replied, still looking adorably crestfallen. They really would have to work on her self-confidence.

"Who's this guy?" Jenner asked, turning toward the squirming dog in Vasco's arms and tickling his ears. She received a hand-licking for her trouble.

"That's Marley," Ty told her. "He's a houseguest, too."

"Welcome, Marley," she replied, laughing.

"You can get off, if you like," Vasco said. "We'll close off."

"It's okay. Beth's got my car. She's picking me up."

"Okay, if you're sure," Ty replied. They had never left her to lock up alone before. "One of us will come back down and set the alarm once you've gone."

"No problem." She turned away upon hearing one of the clients call to her. "Catch you later, Sorrel."

"Yeah, sure." Sorrel watched her walk away. "She seems nice."

"She is," Ty said, sliding an arm around Sorrel's waist. "And in case you're wondering, Beth is her significant other."

"Oh, I see." Ty shared a glance with Vasco, amused when her face flushed bright crimson. "Actually, I wasn't. It's none of my business."

"Liar!" Ty chuckled. "Come on, let's get you upstairs."

"You could have phrased that better, buddy," Vasco remarked, still looking amused.

"Sorrel knows what I meant, don't you, babe?"

"I haven't known what either of you mean since meeting you, if you want the truth. I think you speak a different language to me."

Ty chuckled. "Darlin', you have no idea."

Ty, still with his arm on her waist, guided her to the wide spiral staircase that led to the next floor. Since it was an old building with tall ceilings, there were a lot of stairs, and they were steep. Ty and Vasco thought nothing of flying up and down them twenty times a day, often taking them two steps at a time without feeling the effect. By the time they got to the next level, though, Sorrel was breathing hard.

"This floor is all exercise rooms, for classes and stuff, plus changing rooms, steam rooms and sauna and our office," Ty explained.

"I have to climb another staircase?" she asked, sounding as appalled as she looked. "My thighs are already protesting. Isn't there an elevator?"

"Want me to give you a fireman's lift?" Ty asked, grinning.

"My thighs suddenly feel like they've recovered," she said with another cute blush. "Lead the way, slave driver."

The next flight opened directly onto their living quarters, a high-ceilinged open-plan space with views over the harbor and the entire town. She went to the windows, looked down and gasped with pleasure.

"Some view," she said.

"Yeah, but you don't wanna see the heating bills in winter," Vasco replied, wincing.

"Well, if you will take on these old buildings."

She turned in a circle and took a closer look at her surroundings. She was probably disappointed. They had put all their money into turning the gym into a state-of-the-art masterpiece in chrome, steel

and teak wood. There was no money left for their own space and it
was furnished with a mishmash of castoffs from other times and
places. They both thought it was comfortable enough, given how little
time they got to spend in it. Seeing it now through Sorrel's eyes, he
guessed it missed the feminine touch. He opened his mouth to defend
it, to explain. Then closed it again. It wasn't *that* bad.

"Grab a seat, babe," Ty said. "I guess we could all do with a
drink."

Without waiting for a reply, he went to the kitchen area and
opened beers for himself and Vasco. He figured Sorrel for a white
wine type of girl. It was what she had asked for in the restaurant, but
she'd only had one glass. Another one might help her to relax. She
was strung tighter than a bow. He poured her a decent Chardonnay
and handed her the glass.

"Thanks," she said, looking uneasy.

"Welcome to our humble abode," Vasco said, sending her a
scorching smile as he raised his bottle to her.

"Likewise," Ty said, doing the same thing.

"Thank you." She smiled as she watched Marley slurp noisily
from the water bowl Vasco had put down for him and then
commandeer the most comfortable chair in the place by hurling
himself into it, curling up in a tight ball and claiming squatter's rights.
"It's kind of you to invite me. I didn't realize how badly I needed a
change of scene. I can't think of the last time I took a vacation."

"That's what we figured," Ty replied. "It shows, babe. You work
too hard."

"Listen who's talking. I get the impression you guys put all your
time and energy into this place. And it's not as if you can get away
from it because you live above the shop."

"Sure we do, but it's ours, which makes a difference. Anyway,
we're talking about you, and you're free to relax here." Ty winked at
her. "No one will bother you. And you can ramble around Port
Angeles to your heart's content."

"We take groups out to nature trails and stuff during the week," Vasco told her. "So if you and Marley wanna come along and amble about, you might find that's a cool way to recharge your batteries."

"Just so long as you don't plan on getting me jogging," she replied, narrowing her eyes suspiciously.

"Wouldn't think of it." Vasco blew her a kiss. "Excuse me for a moment. I'll just go down and lock up. Play nice without me."

"Running up and down those stairs will be enough to keep me fit," Sorrel said as she watched Vasco disappear. Marley, who had been sound asleep, cocked his head, jumped for his chair and scampered off after Vasco.

"I think my dog must be fickle," Sorrel said, smiling as she watched him go.

"He's checking out his new territory, is all."

"Well rather him than me. I'm out of the habit of stairs, what with my apartment being on the first floor."

"You'll feel it for a day or two, then you'll be fine."

She appeared dubious. "Easy for you to say."

Ty didn't attempt to break the ensuing silence, contenting himself with focusing a probing gaze on her profile, leaving her to decide what she wanted to say to him. He could tell she had questions. All he knew was that it felt natural and right to have her there, sharing their space. Many women had tried, but Vasco and Ty were too private to take the chance. They both knew from bitter experience that once a woman got her foot in the door, getting her out again was not so easily achieved. If they wanted to play, they did it away from home. Sorrel, on the other hand, had made no effort to infiltrate, and yet here she was, and at their invitation. Go figure.

"I need to understand why I'm here," she finally said, her words echoing his thoughts. "Vasco prevaricated when I asked him. Why are you guys doing so much for me?" She shook her head. "I just don't get it."

"We like you," he replied, because it was the truth. "And you need help with more than just your slogan thief."

"Hmm, I got the impression it was more personal than that. At least for Vasco."

"Possibly, but you would need to ask him about that."

She sighed. "I did. He wouldn't say."

"Okay, here's the deal." Ty scooted across and sat beside her on the settee. "You have so much going for you, so much to offer the world, and it's killing us that you can't see it."

"Oh, come on! You're surrounded by lovely, nubile young women in this place. *Slim,* nubile young women."

"There you go again. You really are hung up on your appearance." He ran a finger down the length of her upper arm, slowly, seductively. "Not many women over the age of twenty have perfect figures." He shrugged. "Not that many under twenty for that matter. Fast food has seen to that. Fucking corn fructose. Don't get me started on the damage it's done. Do you have any idea of the obesity numbers in America? You are not close to being obese. In fact, you're gorgeous."

"Ty!" She shook her head, but a tiny grin invaded her lips. "Now you're just being silly."

"I tell it like I see it."

"Having the perfect body matters to you guys. I get that part. I mean, that's what all those scary machines downstairs do, isn't it?"

"What we do here is encourage our members to make the best of what nature gave them. You could exercise for hours a day but if, say, you have big tits or a large butt, or a big waist, that situation would never change. Those areas would just become more toned, is all. The only way to permanently change your shape is to go to a plastic surgeon, and I wouldn't recommend that in your case." He flicked a finger fleetingly against the outside of one of her breasts, making her gasp. "It would be a crying shame."

"My mom and sister both had their breasts enlarged. I'm sorely tempted to have mine reduced."

"Please don't."

She blinked. "Why should it matter to you?"

"First off, silicone is a real turn off for most men."

"Well, I won't need any of that. Anything but. Mom and Maggie both say they invested in it for themselves, not to attract men."

He elevated a brow. "You believe that?"

"Well, I'm not sure. There's a lot of pressure for women to have…well, sizeable assets. Men, too, for that matter." She giggled. "I get a lot of junk e-mails offering me penile extensions. I'm glad to say that's one area that I don't have to be concerned about."

Ty laughed as he shifted his position, crossing one leg over his opposite thigh. He wondered if she would notice the size of his asset, which had sprung to attention and taken a keen interest in the turn the conversation had taken.

"Sure, I understand the pressure they must have felt, but natural is still better. Your tits are one of your best features. Never let anyone tell you otherwise."

"We are none of us happy with the way we are, is what you're saying?"

"Absolutely." He sent her a slow, sexy smile. "And in your case, darlin', you are pretty near perfect. How to make you understand that, though, that's what Vasco and I have been trying to figure out."

"I know you're just being kind, but it's okay. I'm learning to accept that I don't have a lot going for me physically. Since I inherited money, how I look doesn't seem to make a difference." Her wounded expression damn near killed Ty. He would like to throttle her family, and her ex, for reinforcing her self-doubt. "Everyone wants a part of me now, whereas they couldn't spare me the time of day before."

"Oh, darlin'." Ty shook his head. "Let's take stock of the situation. Apart from your gorgeous tits, what else do you like about yourself?"

"Earth to Ty. I've told you that I hate, despise, and loathe my tits."

"Well, just for the record, Vasco and I don't." He fixed her with a challenging look. "Come on, there must be something you like about yourself."

"Well, I suppose my lower legs are okay, but my thighs are huge, so that leaves out short skirts."

"That's something else about you. You know how to dress to make the best of yourself."

"All women do."

Ty laughed aloud. "Hardly. Okay, anything else?"

"My hair's okay, I suppose." She spread her hands. "But that's about it."

"You've forgotten your complexion, which is fresh and creamy. Your eyes are sensational. You have a tiny waist."

"How do you know that?"

"I put my arm around it just now, remember?"

"Oh, okay, but it's kinda swallowed up by my belly and hips."

"You also have really cute feet," Ty said, shaking his head at her determination to remain negative.

"Feet!"

"Absolutely." He leaned down, tore off one of her killer heels and rubbed the soul of her foot between both of her hands. "Feet are one of *the* most erogenous zones on the human body. Want me to prove it?"

Sorrel leaned her head back and closed her eyes. "Hmm, that *does* feel good."

"I hardly got started yet." Ty continued to rub her foot, pleased to see her gradually relax. "But quite apart from anything else, you have presence."

"Presence?" Her eyes flew open again. "What the heck does that mean?"

"You didn't understand what Vasco meant in the restaurant earlier when he told you never to walk like the hostess?"

"I thought he was kidding. She was gorgeous."

"She was putting on a show. That wasn't how she walks naturally, but you do."

She looked astounded. "I do?"

"Sure. You move with natural elegance. That shit can't be taught. It always comes across as fake, just like when that hostess wiggled her hips and expected a reaction from us. She wasted her time because it did nothing for us. You, on the other hand, have naturally good posture. You'd be amazed how many people don't think about the difference it makes to their appearance if they hold their heads high and shoulders back. They spend a fortune on cosmetics, nips and tucks and a load of other shit, when simple good posture would make way more difference, and costs them nothing."

"I suppose it does." She stared off into the distance. "I've never really thought about it. I guess I started holding myself tall when my tits first started sprouting and I got teased about them. I figured if I breathed in and held myself upright, they would seem smaller. I'd seen other big-breasted women slouching, which drew attention to them."

"There you go. You have natural elegance."

"And a huge butt."

"And that's a bad thing because..."

"Ty, why do I want a backside that's too big for an airplane seat?"

"But perfect for spanking," he said softly.

"What is it with you and Vasco?" She puffed out her cheeks, embarrassed or exasperated, it was hard to tell which. "He kept banging on about spanking."

Ty chuckled. "I guess he didn't tell you."

"Tell me what?"

"No, I didn't." They both turned to see Vasco and Marley appear at the top of the stairs. "And now isn't the time."

"Guys, you're freaking me out here," Sorrel said. "What is it precisely that you haven't told me?"

Chapter Eight

Sorrel was unable to interpret the look that passed between Vasco and Ty. What was it they weren't telling her, and why didn't she feel more wary of them?

"Come on, babe," Vasco said. "I'll show you to your room. You must be beat."

Sorrel met his gaze, and held it. "I'm not going anywhere until you answer my question."

Another look passed between the guys. They both appeared uncomfortable, which ought to have put her on her guard. Instead, she felt safe and protected. It was the damnedest thing.

"We let our true colors show for a minute there. Don't give it another thought."

"Vasco!"

"Best tell her, Vas, before her imagination gets the better of her."

"She might think we brought her here for that purpose."

"She knows better than that."

"How can you be so sure?"

"Er, guys. *She* is in the room and can make up her own mind." She shared a smile between them, enjoying a confidence she seldom experienced because for some reason she felt in control of a situation she didn't entirely understand. Make that didn't even begin to understand.

"Okay darlin', here's the deal." Ty was still seated beside her, watching her closely. Vasco parked his cute butt on the arm of the sofa on her opposite side and fixed her with a searching look. "I don't want you to freak out, but what Ty and I haven't told you is that we're sexual Doms."

"Oh."

"Do you know what that is?" Ty asked.

"I've read *50 Shades.*" She shrugged. "Spanking, domination, all sorts of pain and stuff." She probably should have been appalled, disgusted, outraged…something appropriate like that. She should definitely be frightened. She was shacked up with two guys who had just admitted they enjoyed hurting and humiliating women, hadn't they? Instead she felt intrigued, and very, very interested. "How extraordinary. You don't look like the type to me."

"What do the type look like?" Vasco asked.

"Good point."

"Because of what we are, we can't help noticing…er, shall we say, certain aspects of a woman's anatomy that indicate she would make a good sub," Ty explained. "You exude sensuality. It's one of the first things we noticed about you."

"But we didn't bring you here for that reason," Vasco added quickly. "Don't think that for one moment."

"Why would you?" She shrugged, trying not to show how hurt she was because their interest in her was purely theoretical. She ought to be glad about that. She wasn't big on pain or humiliation. Instead, their attitude only intensified her hatred of her body. "I dare say guys who look the way you do can take your pick from the lovely young things who use your gym."

"Have you forgotten everything we just talked about?" Ty asked in a stirring voice, wagging a finger at her.

"We're not saying we wouldn't like to," Vasco added gently. "Very much indeed, as it happens, but it would be inappropriate. We were called in to help you, not put pressure on you to do things that would probably disgust you."

"Don't I get a say?"

The guys shared another of their speaking looks. "You actually want to play with us?" Vasco asked slowly.

"I didn't say that, but I am interested in what you do." She grinned. "Call it idle curiosity. I always have had an inquisitive mind, and it tends to get me in trouble. Why break the habit of a lifetime?"

"Do you mean that?" Ty asked.

Did she? "Why do you feel the need to behave that way?" she asked instead.

"It fills a need in us. Actually it's a need that's more common than you might think," Vasco said. "The most unlikely people are into BDSM. Dentists, doctors, lawyers, officers of the law. It's a great way to get rid of stress, and since it all happens behind closed doors, between consenting adults, where's the harm in it?"

"But why the need to inflict pain? That's the part I don't get."

"It fuels the need Vas just talked about," Ty replied. "We like to dominate, to have our sub do everything we ask of her without question. But in return her welfare is our responsibility, and a huge one at that. We must ensure she explores her sexual limits but that we don't push her past them, or hurt her in ways she finds unacceptable."

"Not hurt her!" Sorrel thought she must have misheard him. "You want to spank her, whip her, and I don't want to think about what else. How can that not hurt her?"

"Oh, darlin'." Vasco shook his head, his expression smoldering in such a sexy way that dampness seeped between her legs and she had to resist the urge to rub her thighs together in an effort to find relief for the burgeoning need blossoming within her. All this talk about weird practices, done so offhandedly, was definitely making her hot. "The dividing line between pain and pleasure is so thin as to be diaphanous."

"I'll take your word for it."

"A good way to evaluate the relationship between pain and pleasure is to consider them as reward-punishment systems. You associate pleasure with reward, right?" Vasco asked.

Sorrel nodded. "I guess so."

"Right, so it follows pain goes with punishment. Evolutionarily, this makes sense because actions that result in pleasure induce chemicals in the body called endorphins, which are pleasure receptors. How can I explain?" Vasco sent her a heated grin as he took a moment to choose words that, presumably, she would understand. "If the body's hungry, the pleasure it receives from food restores it to a balanced state of replenished energy. Similarly, that theory can be applied to pain because the ability to perceive pain enhances both avoidance and defensive mechanisms necessary for survival. Get it?"

"I suppose." She shook her head. "You guys are really into this stuff, aren't you? You take it seriously."

"It's a serious business," Ty replied. "And just so you know, we're very selective, and we have *never* had a woman from the gym up here with us. Not once. In fact, we've never had any women at all. We go elsewhere if we feel the need to play."

Sorrel widened her eyes. "Why not? I'm sure you'd get plenty of volunteers."

"Just imagine what it would do for our business if word of our predilections got out to the competition," Vasco said. "Not everyone is as broad-minded as you appear to be. Anyway, it's no one else's damned business what we do with our leisure time."

Far from feeling threatened by the high-intensity looks they fixed her with, Sorrel felt turned on in a way she hadn't experienced for years. Perhaps not ever.

"Hang on," she said as a thought occurred to her. "You're both into this lifestyle, I get that, but are you saying you share a woman?"

"Oh yeah!" Ty's smile was lethally sinful. "We like to fuck the same sub."

Sorrel gulped. She would have had trouble selecting one of them over the other, but to take them both…well, she wasn't so sure about that. "At the same time. That means—"

"Now you get why we're so taken with your ass."

"Ty!" Vasco cautioned.

"Sorry, babe. Just sayin'. We're not asking you to do anything. All we're doing is answering your questions because…well, because you asked, and because we trust you to keep it to yourself. You're perfectly safe with us. We promise not to jump your bones during the night if that's what concerns you."

"Spoilsports!"

"You *want* to try it?" Ty asked.

"No, she doesn't," Vasco said.

"Yes, actually, I do," Sorrel said at the same time.

"She's only saying that because she feels obliged to us," Vasco said. "Ignore her. She'll see things differently after a good night's sleep."

"Would you please stop trying to pretend you understand me? You know nothing about me." Sorrel stood up, hands on hips, and glared at Vasco. Sometimes he took the alpha male thing too far. She almost fell over because she only had one shoe on. With a squeal of annoyance she tore the other one off, threw it across the room, and continued to glare at Vasco. "I'm through with people telling me what is or isn't good for me. I've spent my entire life being a good girl." She made rabbit's ears around the words *good girl.* "And look where it's gotten me. Nearly all the men who asked me out spent our dates talking to my tits, not my face." Both men tutted, but she ignored the interruption. "That's why I stopped going out on dates. I only dated Jordi because he was tight with Pete and I thought he was different." She snorted. "Much I knew. The moment he got hired on at Dynasty and got so much attention as a *celebrity* chef, he dumped me so fast my feet didn't touch the ground. One minute we were in a relationship, the next I was sitting by a phone that never rang. It took me a while to figure out he didn't want to be seen with a girlfriend whose figure might imply his food turned people to fat."

"He told you that?" Vasco asked, outraged.

"Not in so many words, but I know it's what he was thinking. Besides, the sex was nothing to write home about, and I can't say I miss it. Not that I have anything to compare his performance to, so it's about time I put that situation right."

"Jordi is the only guy you've had sex with?" Ty asked.

"Yeah." She folded her arms again. "Don't look at me like that. Just because you two sleep around, it doesn't make me prudish because I choose not to."

"We don't think you're prudish, darlin'," Vasco replied with one of those slow, sexy smiles of his that instantly defused her anger. "We love it that you've held back."

"So, what do I have to do to be a sub?" Sorrel felt herself blushing furiously, unable to believe she'd even asked the question. It must be the wine. She never had been a big drinker. But she also knew the wine had absolutely nothing to do with it. She really wanted to get it on with these guys. To let go of her inhibitions and have some fun. Her sex education was woefully inadequate and she had a feeling she'd just landed herself with two of the best teachers in the business. "And what must I call you?"

Vasco answered her question with one of his own. "Why do you want to do this, Sorrel?"

"Why?" She shrugged. "Well, why not? I've never done anything the least bit reckless before. I'm twenty-five years old. It's high time I made up for lost time, don't you think?"

"Oh man!" Ty muttered.

She glanced at him and noticed a huge bulge in the front of his jeans. Well, that made two of them who were turned on by all this talk of sex. Vasco was seated in such a way that she couldn't be sure about him. She recalled how hard he had been when he'd kissed her back in her apartment, which seemed like another world away now. The memory bolstered her confidence, and she was fairly sure he had to be in the mood, too, but was trying to hide the evidence. Fuck it, this was no time to be noble!

"How does it make you feel when you think about submitting to us?"

Her blush deepened but she managed to maintain eye contact with Vasco, sensing it was important to do so. They were both prime alpha males but he appeared to be the one in ultimate charge, and so it was him she needed to convince.

"I feel totally turned on by the thought of both of you touching me." She inhaled sharply. "It's funny, but not once have I worried about exposing my body to you. That's what stopped me dating some of the guys who asked. I thought they would be repulsed." She shared a candid glance between them. "Somehow, I know you two won't be."

"Ah, we're making progress."

Vasco silenced Ty with a look. "If we do this, then you have to obey every command we give you."

"Yes, I know." *Hurry up. I so want to get started.*

"You call us Sir or Master." She nodded. "Say it."

"Yes, Sirs."

"You keep your eyes downcast when addressing us." Sorrel dutifully dropped her gaze to the floor, almost panting with expectation. "We shall tie you up, maybe blindfold or gag you. We will spank your ass and teach you how to embrace the pain. Then we will fuck you. Do you understand?"

She swallowed. "Yes, Sirs."

"Have you sucked cock before?"

"Yes, Sir."

"Hmm," Ty said. "We'll teach you to do it properly."

"Is there anything you won't do?"

"Well, I've never had anal sex. I'm not sure I can—"

"You can and you will. We'll introduce you to it slowly. Anything else?"

"Well, both of you at once." She shook her head. "I like the idea, but I'm not sure I can accommodate you."

"That's something else we'll work up to."

There was a long silence and Sorrel sensed Vasco trying to make up his mind. *Please!* If they rejected her, she would know they hadn't meant what they'd said about liking her body and all her insecurities would come flooding back.

"We need a safe word," he said softly. "Something you will remember easily. If things get too much, you say that word and we stop immediately, without question." She glanced up and discovered Vasco watching her intently. He had unsnapped his jeans and was slowly fisting the most enormous erection. Holy moly, was that all for her? Her eyes widened in frank appreciation. "What word works for you, sweetheart?"

"Backstabbing."

They both grinned. "Fine, backstabbing it is."

Both men stood up and pulled their shirts over their heads. Sorrel drank in the sight of them and gasped. Knowing they had good bodies was one thing. Seeing the evidence with her own eyes was something else entirely. It wasn't a sight many women got to see at close quarters, and yet she had a legitimate excuse to gawp. Sorrel moistened her lips with the tip of her tongue, noticing that Ty had unfastened his jeans too, and sported an erection as large as Vasco's.

Suddenly filled with doubts about her ability to satisfy them, she hastily returned her gaze to their broad-shouldered, godlike bodies. All taut flesh over hard muscle and chiseled abs, they were lean, toned and intoxicatingly, unquestionably male. Their granite chests tapered to narrow waists and slim hips, from which their jeans hung loose. All that coiled strength, rippling muscles shifting and flexing with their movements, and sheer animal vitality, took Sorrel's breath away.

"What must I do?" she asked.

"Go and stand over there," Vasco replied, his voice different now. Hard, commanding, impossible to defy. "Slowly take your dress off for us, but keep your underwear and stockings on and replace your shoes."

Underwear? Thank heavens she'd thought to wear matching bra and panties. Okay, so the bra had half-inch-wide straps. All of her bras did, out of necessity, but at least they made them with pretty lacy cups in larger sizes nowadays. The guys were sitting side by side on the settee, waiting for her to do as she was told, but she hesitated, suddenly full of self-doubt.

"Remember what we told you about keeping us waiting," Ty said, in a firm tone that closely matched Vasco's.

Sorrel hadn't heard either of them speak with so much forcefulness before. Did they have voices they reserved for such situations? She wasn't sure, but she did know it was impossible to ignore their commanding, authoritative presence. Impossible not to react to the dark intensity that formed the bedrock of their expressions. Completely beyond her not to yearn for their respect by doing absolutely anything they asked of her. Already she was beginning to appreciate that pleasing them would bring its own rewards, and she *so* did not want to disappoint them. Her lingering uncertainties evaporated beneath the expectancy in their penetrating gazes, focused squarely and unflinchingly upon her.

Sorrel scampered across the room as though it was on fire.

Chapter Nine

Vasco watched her, wanting her like he couldn't remember wanting a woman quite so desperately ever before. Breaking in a sub was a first for him and Ty. They always played with women who were into the lifestyle and understood the rules. Sorrel, it seemed, was the exception to that rule, just as she was special in so many other ways. Even so, this was *so* not a good idea.

It was the best idea he'd ever had.

He glanced at Ty, suspecting from his expression of fierce expectancy that his thoughts ran along similar lines. Then he returned his attention where it belonged, which was upon Sorrel. It was clear she'd only just realized they had asked her to stand beside a full-length mirror. Even with lowered eyes, she couldn't avoid looking at herself in that mirror as she undressed for them. Nor could she avoid observing their reaction to her, which was Vasco's intention. She needed to get used to this kind of stuff, feel comfortable in her own body, shed her inhibitions, and enjoy giving them a sensual show.

Vasco was already hopelessly addicted to Sorrel. Something about her combination of vulnerability and sassiness had gotten to him. It was their job to make sure she was equally committed to them, and didn't regret what she had committed herself to. The responsibility hung heavily on Vasco's shoulders. It was vital that Sorrel enjoyed herself, learned to embrace pleasure and pain, and that they didn't freak her out by placing too many demands upon her too soon.

No pressure then.

He had an opportunity to help someone to reassess their self-perception, the way he should have hung around and helped Alice.

Perhaps he'd been too young, too angry, to realize that was all Alice had needed. He couldn't change the past, and the guilt he felt at his failure to act would never leave him. But he could do something about the here and now, even if his methods were a tad unorthodox. Sorrel would not become another Alice—not on his watch.

"That's it, baby," Ty said, flashing a slow, appreciative grin. "Let us look at you."

She had lowered the zip at the back of her dress. It fell from her shoulders, revealing wide pink bra straps. She held the dress up against her breasts, looking anxious, unwilling to take that final step.

"Sorrel," Vasco said softly.

His austere tone did the trick. With a reckless shrug she allowed the dress to fall, pooling around her feet. She had already replaced her shoes and stood before them in her pretty pink underwear, hold-up stockings and four-inch heels. She lowered her eyes and folded her hands neatly across her pussy.

"Hold your arms to your sides, darlin'," Ty said. "We need to look at all of you."

She shivered, presumably because she was nervous, and yet was obviously turned on enough to see this thing through. Vasco noticed the insides of her thighs were slick with her own juices, proof positive that she was excited by this game and wanted to play. *Join the club, baby.* Vasco could see large, dark areoles through the fabric of her bra, and heavy nipples that already looked as though they were rock hard fighting against the lace. The sight was driving him crazy, but he resisted the urge to rush things. He also made no comment about how much he approved of what he saw. Instead, he gave her another curt order.

"Open your legs and remove your panties." She gasped, shot him a look that resembled a rabbit caught in headlights, and hesitated. "Do it now, Sorrel."

Slowly, her limbs trembling so violently he was surprised she could still stand, she did as he asked.

"Unacceptable," Ty said.

"What!" Her head shot up, and she forgot all about being subservient.

"No one gave you permission to speak," Vasco said curtly.

Ty, naked now, dashed into the nearest bathroom. Vasco knew why, and what he planned to do. Neither of them liked their women to have pubic hair. Sure enough, Ty returned with a bowl of warm water, shaving foam and a razor. Both men approached her and noticed apprehension in her eyes.

"Keep absolutely still, darlin'," Ty said.

Vasco leaned against the back of a chair, close enough to breathe in Sorrel's fragrance—a combination of sweet perfume and the musky scent of arousal. Ty squatted in front of her spread legs and slowly applied shaving foam to her pubic bone. She gasped, her eyes wide with shock and a tinge of embarrassment, but gamely held her position.

"That's it, babe," Ty said. "Don't move a muscle and let me do my work."

Slowly, carefully, he wielded the razor with long, practiced sweeps, ridding Sorrel of the offending pubes. He moved her labia to the right, getting into the area between her pussy and the tops of her thigh. He grunted with satisfaction before repeating the procedure on the left.

"That should do it."

He carefully wiped her clean of foam, and then dried her with a towel, revealing a sweet, naked pussy with enticing pink lips. Vasco glanced at her face, which was flushed. Her eyes no longer showed anxiety, but burned with sexual awareness. Her legs still trembled, but he was now certain it was only anticipation that made her unsteady.

Ty stood back with Vasco and together they admired his handiwork.

"Now ain't that the prettiest sight you ever did see," Ty said. "You ask me, our little sub is pretty damned anxious for some of this." Ty grabbed his rigid cock in both hands. "What do you think, bud?"

"I think she needs to be chastised first."

"Good point." Ty, still with his gaze focused on Sorrel's cunt, gave her a curt order. "Remove your bra, but leave the stockings and shoes," he said.

Once again she hesitated.

"Each time you're slow to do something we ask of you," Vasco warned, "it will earn you an extra punishment."

Sorrel bit her lip, then reached for the clasp at the back of her bra and unfastened it. Again she hesitated for a beat, then let the straps slip down her arms and threw the garment aside. She blushed crimson but gamely held her position, eyes downcast, legs still spread because they hadn't told her to close them again. At last her glorious tits fell free from their lacy prison, and she didn't attempt to cover them with her hands.

Both men inhaled sharply. The reality exceeded Vasco's expectations. He was a breast man through and through and right then it felt as though all his Christmases had come together. Just as the three of them would soon get to come. But not too soon. He would enjoy tantalizing Sorrel. He was willing to bet she had no willpower whatsoever, or wouldn't have once he and Ty showed her what she was capable of feeling. If her only previous sexual experience had been with the chef jerk, then he figured she didn't have any idea about the strength of the fires burning deep inside of her.

"Come here, Sorrel," Vasco said, holding out a hand.

She walked across to him slowly and slipped her hand into his. Ty fell in on her opposite side and took her other hand.

"Let's take this somewhere more comfortable," Vasco said. "Then it will be time for your first chastisement."

Her breath hitched—a nervous or excited little gurgle at the back of her throat, Vasco was unsure which—but she didn't speak. Vasco opened the door to his bedroom and the three of them walked through it. It was dominated by a huge bed, easily big enough for the three of them, and there were mirrors on every wall.

"Go and stand in the corner with your face to the wall while we decide what to do with you, Sorrel," Vasco said.

He pointed to the corner where he wanted her and she went without argument. Vasco stripped off his jeans and then rummaged in the drawer where he kept his sex toys. What to start Sorrel off with? He held up a flogger, but Ty shook his head. He was probably right. It would be too much for a novice. Ty mouthed the word *hand* to him and Vasco nodded his agreement. He and Ty turned to look at Sorrel, standing obediently in the corner, head bowed, her lovely, virginal backside on open display. *Oh, what a treat!* Vasco pulled a padded stool into the center of the room.

"Come here, Sorrel," he said.

She turned, face flushed, and walked slowly toward them. "Yes, Sirs. What would you like me to do for you?" she asked.

"One of the best ways to enjoy the things we do is to have one or more of your senses taken away," Vasco told her. "I don't want to gag you because that will stop you safewording us if things get too much. And I also think it's too soon to remove your sight. So, that leaves your hands. You will be able to feel, darlin', but you won't be able to touch. Well, not with your hands, anyway, but I'm betting you can do a truckload of damage with those sweet lips of yours."

"I'm counting on it," Ty said, grinning.

"I will do whatever pleases you, Masters." Her voice wobbled, but her resolve clearly did not.

"Damned straight, you will." Vasco picked up the fluffy restraints he'd taken from his drawer and made sure she got a good view of them. "Hands behind your back, sweetheart."

As soon as she complied, Vasco snapped the cuffs into place. "Comfortable?" he asked.

"Yes, Sir. Well, I think so."

"Okay, now it's time for your first punishment. Just remember to relax, and breathe evenly. Don't tense up or you won't get the full benefit. I'm going to spank your butt with the flat of my hand because it will give me pleasure, and you want to please me, don't you, sugar?"

"Yes, Sir, more than anything. But I'm scared."

"Don't be." He ran his hand across her backside with tenderness. It was the first time he had touched her since she'd undressed and he savored the moment. "It's my job to ensure I don't take you too far. It will give you pain to start with, but if you remember to keep your breathing even and are patient, endorphins will run riot in your body and the tingling will transmute to pleasure. Trust me on this."

She swallowed. "I do trust you. I trust you both, otherwise we wouldn't be doing this."

"Kneel down in front of the stool, Sorrel. Lean your torso over it so your tits dangle free on the other side."

She was clumsy with her hands shackled, so he helped her into position. He and Ty shared an appreciative glance at the sight of her unfettered tits swinging beneath her and her ass sticking in the air. Ty slid beneath her, sideways, grasped a handful of breast and sucked the nipple into his mouth. Sorrel gasped and almost elevated into the air.

"Keep still!" Vasco tapped her butt lightly.

"Sorry, Sir, but damn, what Master Ty just did to me felt so good. I wasn't ready for it…didn't know, I—sorry."

Fucking hell, hadn't the chef even bothered to suck her tits? What a selfish jerk.

"Now then, Sorrel. You've been a real bad girl and need to be punished. Do you have anything to ask me?"

Vasco hadn't told her what he needed to hear her say, but had a feeling she already knew. Her next words proved him right.

"Please, Master, I've misbehaved. I need to be chastised."

"What did you do that was so bad, darlin'?"

"I keep having thoughts about you and Master Ty fucking me."

"Hmm, that is bad."

Vasco rubbed the globes of her ass with his hand, warming it, getting fully acquainted with its contours. Her breathing immediately hitched.

"What did I tell you about breathing?"

"Sorry, Master."

He continued to massage her ass until he sensed her breathing becoming deep and regular. Then, without telling her to expect it, he brought his hand down fairly lightly. She jerked and cried out.

"The thought is worse than the reality, babe. Now, let's try it again."

He spanked her several times in quick succession, and this time she held her position and remembered to breathe.

"Oh!" she said, sounding shocked.

"Yeah, that's what I'm talking about." Vasco brought his hand down a little harder, and Sorrel's excited reaction sent his throbbing cock into orbit. "I just knew you'd take to this, sugar. You're doing real well, giving me a lot of pleasure."

Vasco glanced at Ty, who had grasped one of her fleshy tits with both hands and was feeding on the nipple like a man coming off a two-week diet. Vasco needed his share of titty. Besides, she'd had enough punishment for the first time.

"Up you get, babe."

Ty released her breast as Vasco helped her to her feet.

"Okay?" Her glittering eyes told their own story, but Vasco needed to hear her say it.

"I can't believe how much I enjoyed that," she replied, shaking her head in wonderment.

"That," Ty told her, "was just a taste of things to come. What are we gonna do with her next?" he asked Vasco.

"Lay on the bed, darlin', on your back, and raise your hands above your head."

As soon as she'd done so, Ty attached the restraints to the headboard.

"Now ain't that the prettiest picture you ever did see?" Vasco asked as he and Ty looked down at their lovely sub, shackled, naked but for her stockings and shoes, at their complete mercy and clearly more than happy to be that way.

* * * *

Sorrel wondered if she was dreaming, hallucinating, or having one of those out-of-body experiences that were all the rage. Her sore backside told her this was for real, but she still had a problem accepting it really was her—shy, retiring, fading-into-the-background Sorrel—who had attracted two such alpha hunks. And she clearly had attracted them. The size of their erections as they stood at the foot of the bed, absently stroking them as they looked down at her, didn't leave her in any doubt about that. Feeling Vasco's large hand playing with her backside, then spanking it, had been an astonishing experience, once she got the hang of controlling her breathing. Who knew pain could be channeled to be so rewarding?

At first she had been mortified when Ty decided to shave her pussy, without even asking her permission. But as soon as he got started it had been such a turn on that any objections died before she could voice them. And as for the things he did to her breast, biting at the nipple until sensation fizzled through her bloodstream…shit, she was on fire, desperate need fuelling her every conscious thought. But something told her this would be no quick fix. These guys knew what they were doing and liked to take their time.

Having her hands taken out of play had been a bit scary at first, but she already got that it was a great way to learn trust. She had no choice but to surrender control for her welfare to them, which presumably had been Vasco's intention. It felt good. She felt perfectly safe in their care, and was anxious to see what came next.

She wasn't left in ignorance for long. They joined her on the bed, one on either side of her. Ty picked up one of her legs and applied his attention to her foot. He really seemed to have a thing about feet. She was glad because, as he'd rightly pointed out—was it only an hour or so ago, it seemed more like another lifetime—she had delicate little feet. One part of her body she didn't need to apologize for. She gasped when he sucked one of her toes into his mouth, still with a stocking covering it. Vasco leaned in from the other side and covered her lips with his own. His kiss was firm, demanding, searing, and executed with heart-stopping precision, which was pretty much the way he did everything. He coerced her lips apart and plundered her mouth with his tongue with practiced and persuasive assurance, sending her entire body into meltdown. At the same time one of his hands reached for her breasts, probing and molding the flesh with his long, skilful fingers.

Vasco deepened the kiss, at the same time pinching hard at a solidified nipple. Sorrel's cry slipped past their fused lips as passion jolted her tangled perceptions into a heightened state of awareness. She strained against the cuffs, too aroused to remain submissive, not caring if her actions earned her another punishment, half hoping that they would.

Vasco broke the kiss, causing her eyes to fly open and a protest to stall on her lips when she saw he was scowling.

"Did I do something wrong? Master," she added as an afterthought.

Ty was trailing kisses up the inside of her calf, distracting her.

"Your passivity could use some work, darlin', but you're new to this, so we'll make allowances. But, just so you know, the next time you try to take matters into your own hands, it'll earn you a spanking. The same rule applies if you orgasm without permission."

She widened her eyes. "I have to wait for permission to come? How am I supposed to control that need?"

"We'll teach you."

She noticed Vasco nod to Ty, who abandoned her leg. Damn it, just when it was getting interesting.

"Turn onto your hands and knees, darlin'," Vasco said. "I'll help you. The cuffs swivel."

Sorrel got into position, wondering what came next as she supported her weight on her forearms and was acutely conscious of her exposed backside. Surely they weren't going to…her ass? Not so soon. Panic gripped her for a moment, but eased when she felt something cool being rubbed on her nipples, then something else pinching them.

"Nipple clamps," Vasco explained. "You have got *the* most sensitive tits I've ever known, made for these babies, and they'll blow your mind. Are they comfortable?"

Sorrel had read about them, had even thought of investing in some for her solo sex sessions. She was glad now that she'd waited to be introduced to them by experts. "Er, yes. They pinch, but in a good way."

"They restrict the blood flow and increase sensation," Ty explained.

Sorrel wanted to say she already got that part, but wasn't sure if she was supposed to speak unless they asked her a question. Besides, Vasco tugged gently on a chain that connected the clamps and suddenly she had no breath to spare for talking. Pleasure surged through her at the contact and she knew if she rubbed her thighs together she would be able to make herself come. She was very reactive that way. She'd done it to herself more than once after Jordi had left her feeling unfulfilled. It had also happened in public once or twice—in the mall, in a restaurant. She didn't know what had triggered the need, but it was a real turn-on. Perhaps she had a penchant for exhibitionism that the guys had picked up on, accounting for their transitory interest in her.

"Yeah, we know," Vasco said, watching her reaction and seeming very pleased with himself.

Ty slid sideways beneath her face, much as he had when Vasco had been spanking her, but this time he introduced the tip of his cock to her lips. She instinctively opened up for him, and sucked his head into her mouth.

"That's it, babe," Ty said with a soft sigh. "I'm gonna give you a real good face fuck."

Turned on by his words, Sorrel sucked him deeper, enjoying the devastatingly erotic taste of him as she sipped at his arousal, swallowing down a few drops of salty pre-cum. She playfully ran her tongue across his slit, and then down the sensitive underside of his massive cock. She reached his balls and licked them, at the same time tugging at the hairs on them with her teeth.

"Shit, she's a natural at this!" Ty said on a long groan.

She flinched when Vasco's hands started to play with her sore backside, but quickly relaxed into his teasing touch. He ran a finger down the crack between her cheeks, circled it around her anus, but removed it again before she could react.

"So tempting," he muttered, as though speaking to himself.

Before she knew it, his probing fingers were playing with her clit. She almost bit Ty's cock in half when he touched the sensitized nub. Hell, she couldn't take much more of this. They were killing her, their every action intentionally testing her. Vasco slid a couple of fingers into her slick vagina, while his thumb continued to play with her clit. She moaned around Ty's cock but gamely continued to work him, licking him from tip to balls and back again. He pulsated and expanded inside her mouth, groaning words of encouragement.

"That's it, sugar. You keep on doing that." She worked him harder still, empowered to have him at her complete mercy. "Aw, baby, you've got me."

She heard a ripping sound behind her and inwardly rejoiced. Vasco was suiting up. It wouldn't be much longer now. She felt his body heat as his thighs slid onto the outside of hers and the tip of his cock slid into her cunt. Shit, he was big! For a moment she thought she wouldn't be able to accommodation him, and panicked.

"Relax, babe," he said smoothly, reading her thoughts, as always. "You're so desperate to be fucked that you'll take my puny cock with ease."

Puny?

Vasco held her hips in a firm grasp and slammed all the way into her with a smooth upward thrust of his hips, branding her with his cock. At the same moment Ty tugged on the nipple clamp chain and Sorrel screamed around Ty's best friend. Neither man asked if she was in pain. She figured they had to know this was the most glorious torture, making it impossible for her to remain passive. Every cell in her body was aroused and a sizzling current gathered deep in her body, a low pulsating need that was making her crazy. She couldn't hold it. It was asking too much of her. The hell with waiting for permission!

Sorrel clutched desperately at Vasco's cock with the muscles in her vagina, her pulse quickening as desire detonated like an incendiary device. She sucked hard on Ty's throbbing penis, using it to absorb her scream as her orgasm hit—a glittering starburst of pleasure that radiated throughout her body, shaking her to the core.

"Naughty!" Vasco tapped her butt hard, but she could hear the satisfaction in his voice. "I just knew you had it in you to react like that."

"She's greedy is what she is," Ty said, sounding less in control than he had been a few minutes before. "She's got my cock in her mouth, yours in her cunt, and she still ain't satisfied."

"You having fun, babe?" Vasco asked.

"Hmm," was the only answer she could offer with her mouth full.

"Come on, sugar," Ty said. "Let's do this. Make me come for you, darlin'. I'm ready to cream the back of your throat."

Well, Sorrel had had her fun. It seemed only fair that she should return the favor. She worked hard at Ty, while Vasco continued to pummel her pussy, his loaded balls smacking hard against the tops of her thighs with each sortie. Both men were close, she could sense it in their harsh breathing and the way both their cocks were expanding inside of her. Vasco's rubbed the sensitized walls of her cunt, stretching her to capacity until she thought she'd died and gone to heaven. This was exquisite torment in its basest form. Vasco's hot, slick tempo was now reaching a crescendo and, astonishingly, so was she. She was going to come again. She could feel it building deep in her belly and could hardly believe it. She knew some women were capable of multiple orgasms, but had never thought she was one of them. Who knew?

"That's it, darlin', you got me."

Ty thrust himself deeper into her mouth, groaning as he released a thick stream of semen so fast that she struggled to swallow it down quickly enough. She struggled because she was distracted. Vasco was spanking her butt each time he withdrew, then slamming back into her a little harder, a little deeper each time.

"Vasco!" she cried, her voice sounding astounded, desperate, and incredulous all at the same time.

"Yeah, darlin'. I know. Let it go for me."

They exploded at the same time, riding the crest of a rolling breaker as it ebbed and pitched before picking up strength and crashing to shore with a thunderous roar. Vasco's body was a hot prison above hers, his guttural moans, the sound of his fractured breathing, echoing around the room as he shot his load into the condom at precisely the same time as a disturbing thrill rocked Sorrel's world.

Chapter Ten

Ty propped himself up on one elbow and watched Sorrel sleeping, her hair spread across the pillows in a tangle of curls, her face slightly flushed, a half smile forming on her lush lips.

As soon as they had recovered their breath the previous evening they'd carried her off to the shower, and then back to bed, not allowing her to lift a finger to do anything for herself. Ty still couldn't believe what a delightful surprise she had proven to be. They had guessed she was a player, but her willingness to be led into their games, the trust she had put in them by allowing them to spank her and shackle her hands, had blown their minds every bit as comprehensively as she'd blown his dick. Her responsiveness, the way her body came alive for them, had been truly astounding.

The Jerk, as Vasco had christened her ex, was clearly the type who would need a map to find his way around a woman's body, and had selfishly given little thought to Sorrel's needs. No wonder she so lacked self-confidence.

Ty was tempted to move a strand of stray hair away from her face, but didn't want to disturb her. She hadn't moved a muscle when Vasco slid out of bed, responding to Marley's whines from the other room and taking him around the block. Ty got to stay here with their little sub-in-training. Much as his cock wanted to wake her in the traditional manner, she looked way too comfortable for him to do anything so selfish. She mumbled something incoherently in her sleep, turned on her side and collided with his body. Her eyes flew open, filled with panic, presumably because she was used to sleeping alone. Disorientated by sleep, she looked terrified and he thought she might scream.

"Hey, babe," he said, placing a hand gently on her shoulder. "It's only me. You were dreaming."

"Ty." A radiant smile replaced her fear. She sat up and stretched, realized she was naked and quickly darted beneath the covers again. Ty grinned, loving her modesty. Like they hadn't seen it all, and her at her most abandoned, the night before. "What time is it? Where's Vasco? Oh God, I'm rambling." She shook her head. "I'm not used to waking up in the same bed as another person. I've never done it before."

"The Jerk never stayed the night."

"The Jerk?"

"Your ex."

She giggled. "Is that what you call him? No, he never did."

"Idiot!" Ty muttered. "But to answer your questions, it's just before seven and Vasco took Marley for his morning constitutional."

"Seven?" She looked horrified. "It's still the middle of the night."

Ty laughed. "You're not a morning person then?"

"No, more of a night owl."

"Well, we're always up early. We have a business to run."

"Yes, of course. And I feel guilty about Marley. You could have left him for me. He's more used to my body clock."

"No worries. It looked like you were dead to the world." He smiled at her, reached beneath the covers and ran a finger down one of her breasts. "How do you feel?"

"Wonderful," she replied without hesitation. "What you guys did to me, it was…well, unexpected. I never knew I was capable of multiple orgasms."

"There's a hell of a lot you don't know about your sexuality, but we'll teach you, if you'll let us."

"You just got yourself a job, mister."

Ty laughed at her enthusiasm. He was glad that in the cold light of day—still the middle of the night for her—she still felt that way and wasn't embarrassed to talk about it. "Just about everyone is capable of coming multiple times, given the right titillation."

She smiled. "I know that now."

"You're very responsive."

"Hmm, I knew that already." She blushed and told him how she could make herself come in public places, just by having dirty thoughts and rubbing her thighs together. "Are you shocked?"

"Not in the least, nor am I surprised. You were made to enjoy sex, darlin', and it's a crying shame you've missed out on so much for so long. But Vasco and I plan to ensure you make up for lost time."

"I don't want to put you to too much trouble," she said, sending him a flirtatious glance from beneath a thick fringe of lashes.

Flirting, huh. Ty didn't think she was a natural flirt and took that to be a good sign. He returned her glance with a sexy look of his own. "You're in luck, because your sort of problems just happen to be our specialty."

"I'll just bet they are." She stretched and wiggled into a more comfortable position. "You and Vasco seem pretty tight."

"We went through basic training together for the marine corps, hit it off and have hung out ever since."

"What drew you to one another?"

"Hard to say really." Ty shrugged. "We're about as different as it's possible for two guys to be, but they say opposites attract."

"Different in what ways?"

"I grew up in foster homes. Never had a family of my own, so I guess I was always different."

"That's sad. It must have been lonely for you, but take it from me, families aren't all they're cracked up to be."

"I've seen enough of Vasco's to know that."

"What's wrong with his family?"

"Ask him. It's not for me to say."

"Now I'm really intrigued."

"I learned to be self-sufficient at a young age, but was going off the rails, getting in with the wrong crowd because foster parents don't usually give guidance. Mine didn't, anyway, although I hear there are good ones. I was just unlucky."

"So why did you enlist?"

"It was a whim which probably kept me on the straight and narrow. The military is my family now."

"Yes, I heard friends of my dad's say that more than once." She gave a one-shouldered shrug. "I suppose it's inevitable, given what you guys go through together. The amount of faith you have to have in one another's abilities to stay alive."

"True enough. Mind you, the service is also responsible for splitting up families. I don't need to tell you the strain it places upon home life, and I saw a lot of guys in the same position as your dad, going off to serve their country and being rewarded with Dear John letters."

"In my dad's case, it did him a favor, except he never saw it that way. He never did get over my mom. It's a shame, because he was an attractive man and could have done so much better." She shook her head. "Is it any wonder I'm not rushing to play happy families?"

"You don't see yourself with kids one day?"

She shrugged again, a little too casually this time, and broke eye contact. "I'm a bit old fashioned, I suppose. I think love and marriage should come before kids, and there's no husband on the horizon. No, scratch that," she said cynically. "I reckon I could take my pick, now that I have a healthy bank balance, but I'm not going there."

"Hey, don't be sad, darlin'." Ty placed a finger beneath her chin and tilted it up, forcing her to look at him. "It's not allowed."

He pulled her into his arms and kissed her, because he couldn't think of any other way to reassure her. And because he wanted to. He reveled in the feel of her full tits pressed against his chest. He loved playing with a sub in tandem with Vasco, but also enjoyed one-to-one times such as these almost as much. He figured that was why Vasco had left them alone for a while. He was really considerate that way. Deciding to make the most of the opportunity, if she was up for it, he rolled onto his back and pulled her on top of him. She laughed and went willingly. Ty reached for her breasts, dangling enticingly just above his face.

"Good morning, sweethearts," he said, kissing each of them in turn, making her giggle. "Why the hell you don't like these babies is beyond me. And, in case you didn't notice, Vasco and I are already addicted to them." He squeezed the heavy globes to emphasize his point. "Never, ever have them reduced, darlin', and that's an order."

"Yes, Sir."

"Are you gonna let me fuck you awake, sweet thing?"

"Yes, please."

He laughed. "Glad you took a moment to think about it." He reached for a condom in the bedside drawer. "This will have to be quick, I'm afraid. I have a class to take in half an hour."

"Quick is good. I can do quick."

He reached between them to roll the condom down his length. Then he reached for her pussy, finding it already slick with her own juices. He ran his finger through them, then held it to her lips so she could taste herself.

"Can't ever get enough of that vintage," he said, sighing.

"It tastes salty." She canted her head, as though trying to be more specific. "I've never tasted myself before."

"There're a load of things you've never done before, but you will, and pretty damned soon. You've got Vasco and me crazy for you."

"You don't have to say things like that." She looked adorably unsure of herself. "I don't need false compliments."

"No, what you need is to learn how to accept a genuine one," he replied, tapping the outside of her thigh.

"Oh." Now she looked plain confused. "Then thank you."

"You're welcome, and you're also in charge," he said in a thick voice. "You have me at your complete mercy. Do your worst."

He could detect excitement in her eye, unsurprised when she needed no further urging. She used her own fingers to part her slick folds, then lowered herself onto his cock, sinking down slowly and taking all of him inside of her in one fluid movement. She squeezed her thighs around him, closed her eyes and threw her head backwards, groaning with pleasure as he filled her to capacity. Ty clutched one of her breasts, molding the flesh and then lifting his head to bite down on her beaded nipple. She cried out and increased the pace of her movements on top of him, uncoordinated, inexperienced, allowing her emotions to guide her. That was fine with Ty. For this morning, at least, she could be herself. Her lessons would resume later on.

Watching her, feeling her clutching his cock tightly by squeezing her pelvic muscles, an idea occurred to him. Vanilla sex he could do. Hell, there wasn't anything he wouldn't do with Sorrel. But he wanted to try a little experiment first. He abandoned her tits, placed his hands on her waist and when she lifted herself from his cock, ready to sink back down onto it again, he held her clear of it.

"What did I do wrong?" she asked, her eyes flying open.

"Nothing, but I want you to do something for me first."

"Anything, Master."

"Take your weight on your knees, stay clear of my cock, and show me how you make yourself come without touching your cunt with your fingers."

He expected her to get all coy and refuse. Instead her eyes sparkled with excitement and he knew she'd do it. "I need to rub my thighs together."

"Fine, but no touching."

She shuffled a little further back. Ty brought his knees up so she was kneeling at his feet, her thighs brushing against one another. Then she lifted one hand to a breast, closed her eyes and tweaked the nipple hard. She threw her head backwards and rubbed her thighs against one another.

"Shit, you look hot, babe," he said softly. "Are you imagining my cock inside you, or is it Vasco's you're going wild for? Don't worry, darlin', we don't get jealous of one another. You can tell me the truth."

But she had gone somewhere in her mind where he couldn't reach her and he got no response. Instead she made a crooning noise, interspersed with panting, as she rocked her pelvis back and forth, faster as her pleasure built. Then her limbs trembled, her mouth fell open, perspiration trickled between her breasts and she screamed as she came.

"Wow." She opened her dazed eyes, cloudy with the residue of pleasure, and blinked at Ty. "I've never let anyone see me do that before, and it's never been that good before, either."

"You like to be watched, darlin'. That's a good thing."

"I guess so." But she didn't sound too sure.

"You also have really sensitive tits. If you have them reduced, you'll lose a lot of that sensitivity."

"Oh, I hadn't realized that." She shrugged. "Looks like I'm stuck with them then. Some sacrifices are definitely not worth making."

Ty grinned his approval, glad to have been able to dissuade her so easily. Perhaps she didn't dislike them as much as she made out. "Now, where were we?" he asked.

He reached out a hand and she scampered back to her former position. Ty flipped her onto her back and levered himself over her, taking his weight on his forearms.

"Legs over my shoulders," he ordered curtly, shoving a pillow beneath her butt as soon as she was in position. "I'm gonna fuck you hard and deep, babe. Right now, I'm so turned on, so fucking hard, that I can't do it any other way. Watching you bring yourself off almost made me come, too. You are astonishing."

"Please, Ty, hurry. I'm ready again. I know I'm not supposed to make demands, but I feel on fire for wanting you inside me." She giggled. "I must have been a slut in a former life."

"Don't ever call yourself that," he said harshly. "Needing to be fucked and being honest enough to admit it doesn't make you a slut. And you're about to get your wish, darlin'. I'm gonna give you everything I have until you beg for mercy."

"I ought to warn you, that's not likely to happen any time soon."

He kissed the end of her nose. "Music to my ears."

He thrust into her, hard and aggressively, because he knew she wanted it that way. They both did. She groaned as she took his whole length in one greedy grasp of her muscles and moved with him, fast, urgently. The intoxicating friction created by the walls of her pussy branding his cock was so wild he thought he might actually lose control.

"Come on, babe, now we're really fucking. Stay with me, I need to go harder and deeper."

"I want you to. I want all of you, Ty. Please!"

He set a punishing rhythm, conscious of his balls pulling tighter as he strained not to explode too soon. He wanted this to last forever because nothing had ever felt so right before. She was making mewling sounds, whimpering with need as he stroked her sensitive body with long, fast slides of his thick cock. She closed around him tighter still, trembling, on the brink, which was his undoing.

"Let it go, darlin'," he growled. "Let's do this together."

And they did. She screamed, he grunted, as they scaled the pleasure peak together, hitting the summit in perfect harmony.

"Shit, darlin', what have you done to me?" Ty asked, removing her legs from his shoulders and rolling away from her, totally and completely spent.

* * * *

"Well, that was quite a show," Vasco's voice said from the doorway.

Sorrel opened one eye and smiled at him. "Sorry we didn't wait for you," she said. "And thanks for looking out for Marley."

"No problem." He leaned over the bed and kissed her. "Breakfast's up if anyone's interested."

"It's too early," she said, burying her head beneath a pillow.

"She ain't a morning person," Ty said, levering himself athletically from the bed.

Sorrel opened both eyes and watched him with appreciation. He really did have a body to die for, all taut flesh and rippling muscles, not an ounce of excess flesh anywhere to be seen. Vasco, dressed in shorts and a vest, flashed one of his devastating smiles in her direction. He looked unimpeachably and impressively masculine, too.

And unattainable.

Satiated as she was, seeing them in all their intoxicating male splendor made her uneasy, spoiling the afterglow. Their reasons for bringing her here didn't ring true. They seemed to enjoy her body, but they were into health and fitness, and couldn't possibly approve of someone who'd let herself go in the way she had. They had to want something from her. But what?

Sorrel fell asleep again with that question still rattling inside her brain. An orgasm woke her. Shit, she'd brought herself off again, and in her sleep, too. That had never happened before. She must have been dreaming about the guys and what they'd done to her. That would be enough to make any woman come—repeatedly.

She glanced at the clock and groaned. It was gone ten, but felt like she'd only slept for a few minutes since she and Ty got it on. Guiltily, she slipped out of bed. Marley heard her and leapt into the room, all wagging enthusiasm.

"Hey, buddy," she said. "You have a good time with your new pals? Mama sure as hell did."

Marley wagged some more, jumped up onto her lap and licked her hand.

Sorrel spent a long time in the shower, then padded barefoot through the empty apartment to the room that was supposed to be hers. Her bag had been placed on the bed and she rummaged through it for clean clothes. Dressed in Capris, a T-shirt and sneakers, she brushed her wet hair and left it to dry naturally, then wandered into the kitchen, starving. She glanced down and saw a food bowl had been added to the one Vasco had put down for Marley's water. It was obvious he had thought to buy dog chow as well as exercising the little mutt.

"I am a terrible mother," she told Marley, bending to scratch his ears. "I didn't give a thought to your needs."

She straightened up and saw a note on the kitchen surface.

Morning, sleeping beauty, she read. *You looked too comfortable to disturb. Help yourself to breakfast and wander down any time you feel like it. You're bound to find one of us in the office on the floor below you.*

We had fun yesterday.

Love V and T xx

Love? Sorrel felt warmed yet confused by the note, increasingly disturbed by their thoughtfulness because no one other than her father had ever cared about her welfare before. So far this relationship was way too one-sided. She needed to do something for them in return. But what?

She rummaged in their fridge while she mulled the question over, curious to see how they ate. Lots of cold meats, cheeses and bread. Fruit in a bowl on the surface, packets of cereal left out for her to choose from, presumably. Sorrel made herself some tea, ate a bowl of oat bran with a banana sliced on top of it, and wondered what to do with her day. She could wander out and explore, sit here and work, or go downstairs and watch the gym in action. She didn't want to seem as though she was stalking the guys, but they had invited her to go down. But what if people saw her coming from their apartment? Slim, fit people who used the gym. They would realize she was a guest of the owners and probably wonder what they saw in such a fat lump. She might even give the gym a bad name.

"Oh for goodness sake!" she said aloud. "Get over yourself. You're not that important."

Before she could decide what to do, her cell phone rang inside her purse. She reached for it and groaned when she saw her mother's number. There were two missed calls from her, three from Pete and one from Maggie. *Oh, for goodness sake!* She debated whether or not to answer but in the end she did so, knowing she'd get no peace from her family otherwise. She should have expected this, what with Pete having seen her with the guys the night before. She suppressed a giggle, wondering what could have distracted her.

"Hey, Mom," she said.

"There you are, Sorrel. We were on the point of calling the police."

"Why?"

"Why? No one could find you, that's why. We were worried."

I'll just bet you were. "Pete saw me last night."

"Yes, in Dynasty with two strange men. It was thoughtless of you to go there."

"Why?" Sorrel asked for a second time, almost enjoying herself.

"Well, you must have known Jordi would see you, and be upset."

Her mother had always liked Jordi, mostly because he was quasi-famous. "Jordi dumped me, Mom."

Sorrel slipped off one of her sneakers and examined her feet. Ty was right, they were kinda neat. She hadn't thought about that before. Perhaps she'd buy a pretty-colored nail varnish today and paint her toenails for him. She giggled at the thought.

"He needed space to get his career together, but if he wants you back—"

"Whatever gave you that idea?" *Or should that be, whoever?*

"Oh, I think Pete mentioned something. But I know you were keen on Jordi, and you were good together."

"Hmm." There was absolutely no point in arguing.

"Anyway, where are you, darling? Maggie and I called around to your apartment this morning and your bed hadn't been slept in."

"I'm taking a vacation for a few days."

"You didn't mention it."

"It was a spur-of-the-moment thing."

"You should have waited. I know you need a break, that's why I suggested the cruise."

"I'm not going on a cruise, Mom. I would hate every minute of it. And you can tell Maggie I'm not paying for her kids to go to Orlando. They are rude and ungrateful brats who need to be taught some manners."

Sorrel felt empowered. She had never expressed herself so forcefully to anyone—especially her family—before. Who knew the beneficial side-effects of mind-blowing sex? She could tell from the stunned silence from the other end of the phone that she had shocked her mother. Might as well carry on the way she'd started.

"Oh, and tell Pete I have no intention of joining forces with him and Jordi either."

"What's gotten into you, Sorrel?"

Oh, Mom, if only you knew! "Just letting you know where I stand, or rather where all you guys do. I have plans for my inheritance. Besides, it's invested right now."

"Invested? It's the first I've heard of an investment. You should have asked Pete for guidance. You don't know what you're doing financially." *And Pete would make an excellent role model, given his track record.* "Who's been talking to you? Is it those men you were with?" She heard a note of suspicion clashing with her mother's tone of ill-usage. "Who are they anyway? Where did you meet them? Are you with them now? Be careful, they'll manipulate you the moment they smell money. If they haven't already."

"You think that's the only reason two attractive men would take an interest in me?" Anger surged through Sorrel, even though a small part of her wondered if that was the case. She dismissed the idea immediately, feeling guilty for letting it drift into her head. The guys had paid both times they'd eaten out, were entertaining her here at great inconvenience to themselves simply because they thought she needed a break, and hadn't even asked how much she'd inherited. Besides, her mother was the last person to warn her against manipulators. Talk about double standards. But Sorrel had made her point and didn't want to spoil her dreamy mood by arguing. "Gotta run. My friends are calling me."

"Friends? What friends? You don't have any fr—"

Sorrel cut the call and punched the air. She'd stood up for herself and it felt pretty damned good.

"Stay here," she said to Marley. "I don't think dogs are allowed in gyms. Health and safety, or something equally ridiculous." She found a box of dog treats on the counter, obviously purchased by Vasco, and threw a few at Marley. "I'll be right back, baby."

Sorrel's legs ached as she walked cautiously down the steep stairs, but whether those aches were caused by walking up the stairs yesterday, or by several bouts of athletic sex, she couldn't have said. Nor did she much care. The conversation with her mother had shaken her, even if she'd gotten the better of her for the first time ever. But then, conversations with her mother always did. Sorrel admitted to herself that she didn't like her mother, or any of her family, very much. She couldn't help blaming Mom for what happened to her father. If she hadn't broken his heart, perhaps he would have taken more care and not...no, don't go there, she told herself. *What ifs* didn't solve anything. Sorrel should know. What was done was done, and she needed to get over it and move on with her life.

She reached the next floor down and noticed what looked like an aerobics class going on in a large studio, led by Jenner. Sorrel was surprised to see the attendees were all seniors—very active, lively seniors, who appeared to be having a whale of a time. Sorrel felt ashamed of herself. She was pretty sure she couldn't move as athletically as some of them were doing. Jenner caught sight of her, waved and pointed to the office, presumably because she thought Sorrel was looking for the guys.

She peered over the railings and could see parts of the gym on the first floor. It seemed to be fairly full, and most of the machines were in use. Hmm, if she wanted to go outside, she would have to go through that floor, but she didn't have a key card. She would need to interrupt Vasco and Ty, but at least she had a legitimate excuse to do so now and they wouldn't think she was clinging.

The door to the office was slightly open, and she could hear Vasco's voice. He must be on the phone because she couldn't hear anyone else. She didn't mean to eavesdrop, but didn't want to walk in on his conversation, either. So she hovered outside the door, waiting for him to end the call.

"I know the payment's due. I'm asking for a few more days, is all." Pause. "Yes I know I said that before, but this time I mean it. I will know for sure by the weekend." Another pause. "Thanks, I appreciate it."

What was that all about? Sorrel wondered, even though it was none of her business. She pushed the office door open and was astonished to see Vasco resting his head on his arms, as though in despair. He must have sensed her presence because he glanced up, saw who had interrupted him and one of his glorious smiles graced his rugged features.

"Hey, gorgeous," he said. "You're awake."

Chapter Eleven

"Sorry, I didn't mean to interrupt."

"You're not." Vasco shoved the pile of unpaid bills he and Ty took in turns to juggle with beneath a pile of brochures advertising the gym's facilities. "In fact, I was about to come up and check on you."

"You don't need to do that. I know you're busy. I can entertain myself." She crossed her arms, her posture defensive. "I just wanted to ask if I could have a door card, so Marley and I can go out and explore."

"Sure you can. Better yet, I'll give you a guided tour."

"I don't want to tear you away."

"Hey, if you keep pushing me away, I'm gonna start to feel unloved."

He pulled a wounded face, causing Sorrel to laugh and her stance to loosen up. "We can't have that now, can we? Where's Ty, by the way?"

"He's taken our boot camp group out for a jog."

"Boot camp? That sounds scary."

"It's a two-week wake up call for people who need to get in shape and don't get there through gym membership."

"I qualify then."

"No, darlin', you do not." He grasped her shoulders and pulled her against him for a richly deserved kiss. "When will you get it through your cute little head that we like you just the way you are? The only thing you need to do is tone up a little, and you will be sensational. *But,* we are not complaining about the way you look now, and we didn't ask you to come here so we could change anything about you."

"Someone might see us," she said, pulling out of his arms.

"So what? I'm the boss. If I want to kiss the best-looking gal in the gym, that's my prerogative."

Her face flushed. "I'll go grab my purse and Marley."

"I'll go for you, if you don't want to tackle the stairs."

"Vasco, if those seniors can do all those jumping jacks, I can run up a few stairs." She grinned. "Well, walk up at a sedate pace, anyway. Honestly, those guys put me to shame."

"They're certainly lively," Vasco agreed, sounding proud. "And we aim to keep them that way. It'll extend their lives and give them quality time. Use it or lose it. No point getting old if you're too infirm to enjoy your twilight years."

"I guess not."

Sorrel made her way back upstairs and returned a short time later with her purse over her shoulder and Marley tucked under her arm. She looked flushed out of breath. She joined Vasco just as the seniors were pouring out of the studio.

"Hey, Mrs. G. How was the class?" Vasco asked of the very glamorous lady who touched his arm. She wore full war paint and was dressed all in Lycra, complete with leg warmers and headband *a la* Jane Fonda. Vasco's lips quirked. Only Mrs. G. could pull off a look that was thirty years out of date.

"Hard work as always." Mrs. G. wiped non-existent perspiration from her wrinkled brow. "Jenner's an even harder task master than you are, Vasco."

"You lead that class?" Sorrel asked, sounding surprised.

"Whenever I can," Vasco replied without hesitation. "It's a lot of fun. Besides, I hear some of the rudest jokes in the universe from some of those older guys."

"Just because we're getting on a bit, doesn't mean we don't still know how to live." Mrs. G. chuckled as she turned to Sorrel, smiled and tugged at Marley's ears. "And who do we have here?" she asked.

"This is Sorrel, a friend of ours, and Marley. Sorrel, this is Mrs. Gladstone, the star of the seniors' class."

"Glad to meet you," Sorrel said, shaking Mrs. Gladstone's outstretched hand.

"And you, my dear." She squinted myopically at Sorrel. "My, this is a pretty little thing you have here, Vasco. It's about time you had some fun."

"Oh, it's not like that," Sorrel blustered, blushing.

"Of course it is!"

"How the—"

"It shows in your eyes." Mrs. G. laughed at Sorrel's discomfort. "You look as though you've been lit up from within. I'm not so old that I don't remember that feeling. And, let me tell you, if I was twenty…no, make that forty," she said, wincing, "years younger, I'd give you a run for your money for this sexy hunk."

"You're incorrigible, Mrs. G.," Vasco said, laughing.

"And arthritic, and crotchety, and…well, I won't bore you young things with a list of my ailments." She shooed them away. "Off you go, and have fun. Make sure you do everything I would have done at your age."

Vasco winked at her. "Count on it, Mrs. G."

"She seems nice," Sorrel said, looking justifiably bemused.

"She is, but that was her on her best behavior, which means she likes you. Half the old guys in the class are interested in her. She strings them all along quite shamelessly. Whether she gives out, I couldn't say, but it wouldn't surprise me."

Sorrel smiled. "Good for her."

They reached the lower floor, which was busy with the early lunchtime crowd. Vasco felt Sorrel tense up, probably because practically every woman in the place was young, and doing skimpy Lycra justice. Vasco wanted to tell her they did nothing for him, but her neuroses about her appearance were too deeply ingrained for her to believe it. He and Ty had their work cut out for them. It didn't help when one of the prettiest saw him, stopped leg-pressing and wafted up to him.

"Hey, Vasco. Where you been hiding?"

"How you doing, Sonia?"

"Still on for tonight?"

"Seven o'clock."

Sonia glanced at Sorrel, appeared to dismiss her as being insignificant, and refocused a hungry gaze on Vasco. "I'll be there."

"You have a date tonight?" Sorrel asked as they moved toward the back door.

"Yeah, with a dozen women."

"I beg your pardon."

Vasco suppressed a grin. It was so easy to wind her up, but the devastation in her expression she was trying hard not to reveal prevented him from keeping up the tease. "I run a self-defense class for women," he said. "Sonia attends."

"Seniors, boot camp, self-defense," she remarked, her expression clearing as Vasco swiped his card and held the rear door open for her. "You sure believe in diversifying."

They walked outside and she put Marley down.

"This is your card," he said, handing her the one he'd just used. "It works on the front door and this one."

"Thanks."

"And as for diversifying, we have to do whatever's necessary to attract members. There is keen competition in this area and since we're not in the best part of town, we have to try and be different."

"Yes, I would imagine you do."

"That's why this particular boot camp course is so important. We have a local business sniffing around, looking for corporate membership of a local gym, and we won't be their first choice. But one of the women on this course is PA to the guy who makes the decisions. If she sends back a good report, we just might persuade

them to come to us, rather than one of the better-established joints."
Please God that we do.

She sent him a curious sideways glance. "Is it that important to you? You seem kinda tense about it."

"Long day, plus a certain someone kept me up past my usual bedtime last time."

Sorrel tossed her head. "I didn't hear you complaining."

"No, ma'am!" He grasped her arm. "Come on, I'll show you the better parts of town."

"Lead on. There's a pier and a harbor, isn't there?"

"Yep, right this way."

They strolled for about half an hour, with Sorrel's hand linked through his arm while Vasco pointed out the sights. There were a thousand and one other things he ought to be doing, but nowhere else he'd rather be. It felt a bit like playing hooky, but he figured he'd earned the right.

"How do you feel?" he asked. "I know you enjoyed yourself last night—"

"That obvious, was it?" she asked with a self-deprecating little laugh.

"You're very uninhibited when you have sex," he said, lowering his voice to a seductive purr. "That's a good thing. I just love those cute little mewling sounds you make just before you come."

"I didn't know I was...uninhibited, that is. You guys must take some of the credit for that. It was never that way with Jordi."

Vasco screwed up his nose. "I hope we can service you better than that jerk."

Sorrel laughed. "You make yourself sound like an auto mechanic."

"Yeah." He flashed a wicked smile. "And I promise to keep your motor running."

She playfully thumped his bicep. "That is *so* cheesy."

"But true," he said with an unrepentant smile. "We have our reputations to maintain."

Behave!"

"Not a chance. Speaking of which, Ty tells me you can make yourself come." He sent her a smoldering grin. "I'd pay good money to see that."

"For you, there's no charge."

"Why, thank you. But how did you discover you could do it?"

"Self-preservation."

"Because the jerk left you unsatisfied?"

"Hmm, and you know what they say. The best orgasms a girl has are when she's alone." She glanced up at him. "Up until last night, I'd always thought that was true."

"Shit, Sorrel, look what you've done to me." He pointed down at the erection tenting his shorts. "Come and sit over here." He directed them to a bench in a quiet part of the little park they'd been walking in. He took Marley from her, freeing her hands. "Do it for me now, darlin'. Rub those luscious thighs together and make yourself come."

"What here, in the open?" She looked shocked. "Someone might see."

"They might, which makes it all the more exciting. Come on, don't make me ask you again," he said, switching to Dom mode.

"All right, Sir, but I need to touch my tits."

Vasco swallowed. "Go right ahead."

She closed her eyes, threw her head back and rubbed her thighs together. A hand drifted beneath her T-shirt, obviously pinching a nipple through the fabric of her bra. Watching her, Vasco felt as though his entire body was about to implode. He had never seen a sexier sight in his entire, very extensive experience of the female species. A pretty girl giving herself pleasure in a public place was beyond erotic. His cock throbbed and he absently rubbed it as he watched her lift her pelvis from the bench, slowly at first, and then with increasing force.

"Fucking hell, Sorrel, this is one huge turn-on. I've never seen a woman do anything like it before. Keep going, baby. You are so fucking sensual, I think I might come in my pants just watching you."

It was either his words or her imagination that spurred her on. At first she kept opening her eyes, making sure no one was watching. Now she was in the zone and didn't appear to give a shit if the entire population of the city was looking on. Was she a girl after his own heart, or what? Thoughts of what the three of them could do together on some of the machines in the gym filtered through his brain, adding to the pain he was getting from his swollen cock.

"That's it, darlin'." He reached out and touched her other breast, pinching the nipple with considerable force. She gasped, her eyes flew open, the pupils hazy and dilated. Her pelvic movements gathered momentum, rocking the entire bench as she neared the end game. Vasco squeezed her tit harder still and she cried out loudly enough to frighten a flock of pigeons pecking at the grass near their feet into flight as she shuddered to a climax.

"Holy fuck!" Vasco said in an awed tone.

"How was that for you, Sir?" she asked, biting her lower lip and sending him a wicked grin.

"Sen-fucking-sensational, but look at the state of me." He pointed again to his erection. "I have a class to lead in an hour. How the fuck am I supposed to do that with this baby bobbing about?"

"Want me to do something about that for you before then?"

"I thought you'd never ask." He grabbed her hand and all but dragged her back to the gym. "Come on!"

He took her up to the second floor and into his office, closing and locking the door behind him. Marley, presumably sensing their urgency and knowing their attention wasn't for him, scuttled into a corner and curled in a ball with a martyred sigh.

"Take everything off, and lean over the desk," he said curtly, clearing it of all papers with one sweep of his hand. "I'm gonna spank your butt for being such a tease."

He picked up a ruler and flexed it against his palm while she stepped out of her clothes with indecent haste. He stripped off too, sighing with relief when his raging hard-on sprang free from his underwear, earning him some relief from the consistent throb. Shit, he needed to fuck her, and fuck her hard, he thought, watching as she got into position on the desk.

"Aw, sweet darlin'." He ran a hand gently over her backside. "Your butt is the stuff of dreams. Will you let me spank you?"

"Yes, Sir. You need to. I was a real bad girl. I made myself come outside in the park where anyone might have seen."

"You damned near made me come, too. I haven't lost control like that since I was a horny teenager."

He removed his hand and brought the ruler down over her ass quite hard, figuring she was turned on enough to withstand the pain. She whimpered, but held her position, so he repeated the punishment.

"Your ass is the cutest shade of pink," he told her, having slapped it a half dozen times. "Now, I'm gonna take a little bite. Hold perfectly still, honey. Remember to breathe slowly and you'll enjoy it."

"I'm enjoying this already, Sir. I so love it when you get all masterful."

"Get used to it, sugar. You ain't seen nothing yet."

He sucked and then bit both buttocks, careful not to break the skin, sensing she was relaxed enough to feel the benefit. She cried out, which was unacceptable. He grabbed one of the small, flimsy towels he kept in the office for use when he was called from a class to take a call, and tied it around her mouth. Her eyes widened, but Vasco figured it was with excitement, not fear. He couldn't remember the last time he'd been so turned on, so ready to fuck a woman's brains out. Not just any woman, he mentally corrected himself, but Sorrel. Only she could make him feel this way, and the intensity of those feelings scared him shitless, mainly because he didn't know what to make of them.

"Spread your legs," he ordered curtly.

She did as he asked, her juices flowing onto the surface of the desk. He'd punish her for that at a later time. God, he'd love to take her ass, but that was a work in progress to be tackled when they had more time to introduce her to that particular pleasure. Later tonight perhaps. It was probably too soon, but she had taken to everything they'd done to her so far, embracing the pain, with enthusiasm and excitement. Her body was designed for mortal sin, and who were he and Ty to deny her?

"Shit!" He was on the point of slamming into her from behind. "No condoms down here. Are you on the pill, darlin'? Can I come inside you? I'm clean. So is Ty. You won't catch anything from either of us."

She nodded, which was all the encouragement Vasco needed.

He stood behind her, between her splayed legs, and grabbed her hips to pull her closer. She was leaning on her elbows, her nipples rubbing against the surface of the desk, looking so damned adorable Vasco nearly lost his mind. He took one hand from her hips and grasped his cock, pushing the tip into her welcoming warmth and sliding all the way home with one smooth, fluid gyration of his hips. Vasco groaned with pleasure. She was so tight she was messing with his frigging mind, to say nothing of his control, but after what she'd just done for him in the park, he figured he was permitted to make this quick.

Without a rubber, the friction made by his cock against the sensitive walls of her pussy was *the* most intoxicating torment. He closed his eyes and groaned. The little witch gurgled around her gag and then pushed back to encourage him deeper. Shit, but she was insatiable! He found it hard to believe that someone with her needs had survived for so long on a do-it-yourself basis. He didn't count the jerk, who had clearly only thought about himself, the selfish bastard. Well, he and Ty would make it up to her, if she didn't wear them out in the process—a very real possibility.

Vasco circled his hips and thrashed into her, figuring there were worse ways to die.

"That's it, babe," he said, grunting with the effort he put into it. "Now you've got all of my cock inside you and we're really fucking."

He set a punishing rhythm and she stayed with him every step of the way. Her pussy clenched around his length and her breathing fractured. Before he could forbid it, she exploded, her body rocked by a series of virulent tremors. Vasco continued to give her what she needed—hard, brutally, until the quivering receded. He tried to total up how many orgasms she'd had in the past less-than-twenty-four hours, but gave up. He had no way of knowing how often she'd done that thing with her thighs, but he did know he could improve on her self-induced variety of orgasm and picked up the pace again with that objective in mind.

"You liking this, darlin'? I know you can't answer me, but shake your head if it gets too much for you."

No shake, but a vigorous nod. Vasco chucked.

"That's my good girl," he said in a husky voice, straightening up so he could drive harder and deeper into her. "I can't wait to see you taking my cock and Ty's at the same time." She shuddered. "Yeah, you like that idea, don't you, sugar?" He leaned over and took a soft nip at her shoulder. "Two big cocks fucking you senseless is all you can think about. Well, you're just gonna have to make the best of mine for now." He felt his balls pull tighter. "Come on, honey, give it up for me. I want you to come now, and come hard. Can you do that for me?"

He reached for one of his tits and squeezed it brutally as he sheathed himself into her slick warmth. Her pussy clenched and she thrashed against him, setting him off. Vasco shot his load deep inside her, eyes closed, head thrown back, a soft growl rumbling in his throat as he eased his aching need for her.

Temporarily.

Vasco waited a moment for his heart rate to slow, then withdrew, pulling Sorrel up from the desk. He untied the gag and took her into his arms to kiss her, almost chastely.

"Hey," he said. "Was that too rough for you?"

She sent him a vibrant smile. "Is there such a thing?"

Vasco chuckled. "I just knew you were one of us."

"Which is more than I knew."

"Yeah, well, Ty and I will spend the night proving it to you, if you'll let us."

"Hmm, I don't think I have anything better to do."

"Witch!" He batted her ass hard, then let her go so he could fetch a towel and clean them both up. "Get dressed, hon, and we can shower quickly upstairs."

"What about your class?"

"Aw, shit!" He glanced at the clock, pulled a rueful face and reached for the phone. As he did so, she picked up the papers he'd thrown on the floor and stacked them neatly back on the desk. She grinned when she saw her juices drying on the edge of the desk, sent him an apologetic smile and a little shrug, and wiped them away with a towel.

"Hey, Jenner," Vasco said when his manager answered the house phone. "I'm gonna be a few minutes late for my class. Get Sally to start them on warm up stretches and I'll be there by the time they're ready to go."

"I've made you late," Sorrel said when he hung up.

"It's okay. We have a couple of phys ed interns on staff for the summer. One of them can start the class."

They were both dressed again. Vasco reached for Marley, still snoozing in the corner, and the three of them left the office. Vasco figured if they were seen, their faces would give them away, but right now he didn't give a shit. In the event, they made it upstairs without meeting anyone. Once again their clothes were off in seconds and they shared a shower. Vasco would so like to take his time, soap her all over, and go for an action replay—slower this time, with Sorrel cuffed to the bed, blindfolded, and perhaps gagged, too, while she took a well-deserved whipping. But he couldn't skip his class. Even so, there was one thing he needed to do first.

"Don't dress yet," he said, stepping from the shower and wrapping Sorrel in a large, fluffy towel.

With a towel around his own waist, he led her to his bedroom and ordered her to lay face down on the bed. Then he carefully applied lube to the crack in her butt, circling his finger around her anus.

"I'm gonna fix you up with a butt plug," he explained. "Now don't fight against me, sugar. You know I wouldn't do this if I didn't think you'd take to it like a natural, don't you?"

"Yes," she replied breathlessly.

"Then don't tense up against my finger. Let me in, darlin'."

He spoke in a softly persuasive tone designed to imbue her with confidence. It worked wonders. She wanted to try this—no question. The next time his slick digit slid into her backside without meeting opposition. He moved it around, causing Sorrel to let out a sharp exclamation of surprise.

"Yes," he said, satisfaction in his tone as he leaned in to kiss one buttock. "Already you're getting it. Good girl."

With his free hand, he reached for the small plug he'd already lubed, removed his finger and slowly inserted the plug in its place. She gasped again, and tried to fight him.

"Don't!" He tapped her butt hard. "Let me do my work. This'll distend you, darlin', and get you ready for what I'm gonna do to you later. You just rest up for the next few hours. Lay here, think about Ty and me, and regain your strength. You're sure as heck gonna need it."

The plug slid deeper, and Vasco gently eased it into position.

"There you go." He leaned down and kissed each buttock. "Shit, I wish I could stay and fuck you again. Never mind, we'll catch up later."

"How do I walk about with this thing in?" she asked.

"Clench your buttocks together, sweet thing. It'll stay. Is it comfortable?"

"It feels intrusive, but not in a bad way."

"That's good, real good. It's got oil inside it and when it heats up, so will you." Vasco chuckled. "Not that you ain't already red hot, but this will take you to another dimension." He told her to stay as she was and fixed her with a little harness to keep it in place. "Here, put this on and you're all set." He threw her a pink T-shirt with Body Language emblazoned across the front. "I don't expect you to be wearing anything else when we get back."

"I need to wear a bra."

"No you don't." He slapped one buttock. "What did we discuss about arguing with me when I tell you to do something?"

"Sorry, Sir."

"That's better. When you're up here, you wear what we tell you to, which will most likely be not very much at all."

She giggled. "This is fun," she said.

"Yeah, that's kinda the idea." He ran a hand possessively over her backside, filled with longing that he couldn't act upon quite yet. "You just need to leave your inhibitions behind, not that you seem to have many, and remember that nothing which happens between consenting adults is taboo."

"I'll bear that in mind," she said, wiggling her butt at him.

Vasco groaned, deciding she would pay for being such a provocative little tease when he had the time to deal with her. "I gotta run. Be a good girl, and don't bring yourself off too often. Get some rest, and we'll attend to your needs, especially the ones you don't know about yet, later."

"Yes, Sir," she said, canting her head sideways from her position, still on her front, and sending him a sexy smile, one hand beneath her tweaking a fat nipple. "I'll be sure to do that."

"Later, babe."

He blew her a kiss from the doorway, and forced himself to leave her.

Chapter Twelve

Sorrel could barely keep her eyes open, unable to recall the last time she'd felt so tired. Still, there were different types of tired, she supposed, and she hadn't played these sorts of energetic games before, so she figured she'd earned her tiredness. A wide smile invaded her lips as she thought about the games in question. Who knew rough sex could be so rewarding? The guys were right about her. She had taken to it, thrown herself wholeheartedly into their games, and really gotten into the spirit of things. They'd been able to tell she would the moment they set eyes on her. How? Did she wear a neon sign that told the world she enjoyed sex?

She liked to orgasm—she masturbated daily, at least once—which presumably meant she had a high sex drive. But they weren't aware of that. No one was. It was way too personal to share, and no one's business but her own. It had been enough for her—up until now. Now she knew better. The pleasure she took from flying solo was nothing compared to what the guys had shown her, and there would be no going back to lonely nights cuddled up to an impersonal vibrator.

What she would do instead, she had yet to conjecture. She wasn't stupid enough to imagine this gig with the guys would last for long, but she'd cross that bridge when she came to it. First off, she needed to complete her erotic education. She had lost time to make up for, and had been lucky enough to land herself with two of the best teachers on the planet. She wasn't about to waste that opportunity.

The plug thingy in her backside was already starting to heat up. She wiggled about and the warmth spread, making it feel like her entire body was glowing. Was she really going to let them fuck her ass—fuck her together? Asked that question as recently as one day ago and her answer would have been a prudish *hell no!* But she was no longer the same person and the new, improved, liberated Sorrel wouldn't hesitate. Whenever they got all masterful with her, it filled her with determination to move heaven and earth to please them.

She couldn't believe she'd brought herself off in the park like that. In broad daylight, with people wandering about just yards away from them. It was wild! She giggled when she recalled how impressed Vasco had been. She had a feeling he didn't impress easily, and the way he'd fucked her over his desk…well, his cock was so big she'd thought he might split her in two. She fidgeted into a more comfortable position, idly playing with her nipples. Hell, she was one lucky girl and, for as long as it lasted, which wouldn't be more than a few days because she had a life to get back to, she would make the most of every moment.

She drifted off to sleep, idly wondering about all those bills she'd collected from the office floor. The ones he'd hidden when she'd first walked into the office. Some of them looked overdue, but then that was how businesses ran, wasn't it? Unlike her, who paid her bills the moment they because due, business owners left it until the last minute. She'd learned that much from hearing Jordi talk to the owners of the restaurant he worked at before Dynasty nabbed him.

Sorrel slept for over an hour, feeling refreshed and invigorated when she awoke. She sat up and stretched, wincing because she felt sore in places, especially the muscles in her legs from using the stairs. The butt plug, on the other hand, continued to give pleasure.

Marley, obviously sensing she was awake, appeared at the foot of the bed, wagging.

"Hey, buddy, I hope you don't wanna go out yet, 'cause I have strict orders not to dress. Besides, I can't go out with this gorgeous thing up my ass." She wiggled around and felt that nice glow getting…well, glowier. "I'm sure the guys won't be long and I expect one of them will help you do the necessary."

Marley wagged, but didn't seem in urgent need of any doggy facilities. Sorrel climbed from the bed slowly, wondering how it would feel to walk about with the plug in situ. She took a few cautious steps to the bathroom, pulling aside the strap on the harness that fitted between her legs so she could pee. The plug didn't budge, but felt pleasantly intrusive. Sorrel brushed her hair and examined her reflection critically. Her face was flushed and her eyes glowed with what she could only describe as carnal awareness. She giggled at the old-fashioned phrase, wondering if that was what Mrs. G. had seen in her. Sorrel didn't care if the whole world saw it. For the first time in her life, she was thinking about no one except herself, and she was having a ball. Well, several of them, if she was going to be pedantic, she thought, giggling again.

She grabbed the T-shirt Vasco had ordered her to wear and pulled it over her nakedness. It was large and long so she jauntily tied the ends around her waist, revealing her lower half covered only in a harness. Where had she found the courage to display her lumpiness? Her unfettered tits pressed against the fabric, the nipples hard, the areolas raised and visible. She looked hot, if she did say so herself, and for the first time in forever Sorrel didn't stop to think about all the bits of her body she didn't like. The guys wanted to play games with her. Fine. Let the future take care of itself.

Sorrel wandered into the main room, wondering what to do with herself. Working on her slogans held no appeal, nor did reading or watching TV. She made herself some tea, thinking it was less than an hour before the guys were due to return. Presumably they had to eat, and she enjoyed cooking. Grinning, she decided to surprise them.

She discovered chicken in the freezer—organic, of course—and set it in the microwave to defrost. She hummed to herself, wondering if there was another woman in the world today setting about cooking a meal, wearing a harness over her pussy, a butt plug, and not a lot else. She felt sorry for the majority of the population who weren't, thinking they didn't know what they were missing.

Rummaging in cupboards, Sorrel assembled the ingredients for a stir-fry and set about making a salad, using extra virgin olive oil and high-end Balsamic vinegar to make a dressing. When the guys came pounding up the stairs half an hour later, the table was set with candles in its center, a bottle of red was open and breathing on the counter, and the aroma of spicy food filled the space, hopefully setting their taste buds alight.

"Shit, will you look at that?" Ty stooped dead at the top of the stairs, absently fondling Marley's ears when the dog launched himself at his legs in a frenzy of enthusiastic wagging. His gaze remained fixed upon Sorrel. "What you done to our little gal, Vas?"

"Not a sight you see every day, is it?" Vasco replied, sounding proud.

"Hi, guys," Sorrel said, turning from the stove, spatula in hand. "Your timing's perfect. Go and wash up. Dinner's ready."

"Hey, you didn't need to do that," Vasco said, stepping up to kiss her.

"I wanted to. I like cooking."

"It smells divine," Ty said, taking his turn for a kiss. "But not as good as you look."

"What, this old thing?" She grinned as she indicated her near-naked body with the spatula and gave them a twirl. "I've had it years. It's just something I threw on."

Both guys chuckled, and a short time later they sat together to eat, one on either side of Sorrel.

"How's the plug, darlin'?" Vasco asked, pouring her a glass of wine.

"It's mine!" Sorrel cried possessively. "I hope you're not thinking of trying to take it from me."

The guys shared a look and laughed. "We might be able to improve on that," Ty said.

"Hmm." She treated them to a smug smile. "I sure as hell hope so."

"I hear you did your party trick for Vasco out in the park," Ty said. "Never seen my buddy half so steamed up about anything before."

"It was fun." Sorrel felt empowered, just by the admiration she saw in their expressions. "He fucked me in your office afterwards and made himself late for class. I hope the teacher didn't punish him."

Vasco leaned in and growled at her. "I'll punish you again later. Prepare yourself. There's nothing I like better than laying into that sweet ass of yours with a ruler."

"I would have liked to have seen that," Ty said, pouting.

"You can do it to me if you want to," Sorrel said, touching Ty's arm. "Don't feel left out."

"Fucking straight, I can," he replied, lowering his head and growling the words into her hair.

"This food is delicious, babe," Vasco said, helping himself to seconds.

"Why, thank you."

Once they'd finished, they insisted that Sorrel stay where she was while Ty cleared away and Vasco took Marley outside.

"Vasco told you he has his self-defense class tonight?" Ty asked.

"Yeah, that sounds like a worthwhile thing to do."

"It's his personal project. He thinks all women need to be able to protect themselves in this day and age."

"He's probably right about that. Me, I rely on mace, but it would be nice to know a few moves, just in case."

"Join the class."

She thought of ultra-slim, ultra-sexy Sonia. "Perhaps I will, but not tonight. My muscles are protesting enough as it is. The stairs, the sex…" She shrugged. "It's all new."

Vasco returned with Marley. "Okay," he said. "I gotta go and show these ladies how to kick ass. When I get back we'll think up a few moves of our own, the three of us." He kissed the end of Sorrel's nose. "Play nice without me, children."

Vasco bounded back down the stairs with enough energy to make Sorrel feel tired just watching him. Ty took her hand and led her to a sofa that overlooked the view of the city. She sat in the corner, full of anticipation. Ty would make a move on her, surely.

"Ain't gonna happen, babe," he said chuckling, correctly interpreting her thoughts. Again. "Vas and I want you together tonight."

Sorrel was proud of herself for not whining. Ty sat beside her, lifted her legs from the floor, forcing her to swivel in his direction. Then he rested her feet in his lap and started to massage them so expertly that she closed her eyes and felt herself floating.

"Oh boy!" she murmured.

"You been getting hassled by your family?" he asked.

"Hmm. I turned my phone off in the end. I don't want to talk to them."

"They know where you are?"

"Nope. Oh God, Ty, that feels almost orgasmic."

"Almost? Hmm, we'll have to do better than that, but not yet. Do not rub those thighs together, Sorrel, or there will be consequences. We want you desperate by the time we're ready for you."

"Then I've peaked too soon."

"Just relax, honey. You need this more than you think."

Sorrel's head fell back, her eyes closed. The only sound in the room was Marley's snores and her occasional groan of pleasure as Ty dug his thumbs into her insteps and massaged her into a better place and time.

She must have actually fallen asleep because Vasco's voice, asking what he'd missed, woke her.

"Party time," Ty said. "Thank fuck for that."

Sorrel felt wide awake in an instant.

"Stand up, baby, and lose the T-shirt," Vasco said in the deep, authoritative tone he used in these situations—the one that sent shivers down Sorrel's spine and made her pussy leak like a faulty faucet.

Her legs trembled as she stood, but she managed to do as he asked. Ty approached and fastened a collar around her neck. Nipple clamps were attached to a ring at the front of it on very short chains. He lubed her areolas and attached the clovers. Each time she moved her head backwards it put pressure on her nipples.

"Okay?" Ty asked. "That's quite an advanced piece of kit, but we figured you could take it."

"If feels like my body's on fire." Anticipation consumed her as she observed the passion, the approval, in their eyes. "I love it!"

"Told you," Vasco said smugly.

Ty stood in front of her, something in his hand. That something turned out to be a small vibrator, much smaller than the ones she owned. She figured out why when he moved the harness aside and slid it into her cunt, turned onto a low speed. She felt full to capacity because she still had the butt plug in.

"Now you've got two cocks inside of you, darlin'," Vasco said. "How does it feel?"

"I'll never be able to take the two of you," she said, disappointment and panic vying inside if her. "You're way too big."

"You'd be surprised," Vasco said. "Just trust us to know what's right for you. How does your butt feel? Is it too sore for another chastisement?"

"Hell, no! That I *can* take. Especially with the plug. I think that'll make it feel even more sensual."

"Told you she was a quick study," Ty said, pride in his tone.

"You do the honors, buddy," Vasco said.

"Hands and knees, Sorrel," Ty said curtly.

She scrabbled into position, tugging on the nipple clamps several times when she forgot to move her head cautiously. She heard the guys moving about behind her, but had no idea what they planned to do to her. They took their sweet time deciding and the expectation was slowly killing her.

"Ask me nicely, honey," Ty said.

"Please, Sir. I need to be reprimanded. I did bad things today." Her juices flowed even more freely when a hand reached beneath her and switched the vibrator up a notch, pausing to tug a couple of times on the nipple chain before it removed itself. "I made myself come in a public place *and* I made Vas late for his class because he was busy fucking me over his desk."

"That was a bad thing to do, Sorrel. Are you sorry?"

"No, Master Ty. Master Vasco made me so hot that I couldn't help myself."

"Then I guess I'm gonna have to whip the badness out of you, honey."

Something with more than one thong came down across her ass with considerable force. She cried out, with shock rather than pain, waiting for that magical moment when the stinging sensation became pleasurable. It had barely done so before the punishment was repeated, and then again, and again.

"That's a good girl."

She sensed Ty on his knees behind her, touching her sore backside, kissing it, nipping at it with his teeth. She caught sight of Vasco in the periphery of her vision, stark naked, laying full length beside her. One elbow rested on the floor and his head was propped on his splayed hand as he watched her and Ty intently. He was lazily running a hand up and down his erection, amusement in his expression, presumably because he could tell how much she was enjoying herself. Well, that was kind of the point, wasn't it? What was it he'd said about the dividing line between pleasure and pain? Whatever it was, she was a convert.

"I think she's learned her lesson, Ty?" he said.

"Yeah, up you get, babe. Careful not to move your head too fast. We'll take this into the bedroom."

Sorrel was trembling with such keen anticipation that she didn't think her legs would carry her that far. Vasco appeared to realize it too, and solved the problem by sweeping her from the floor, into his strong arms, and carrying her the short distance. She wanted to warn him that she was too heavy and that he'd probably put his back out, but he didn't seem to struggle at all. She was placed back on the floor again once they reached the bedroom. One pair of hands removed the harness, another took away her toys. She let out a moan of protest when the butt plug was removed, which caused the guys to chuckle. They helped her onto the bed, still wearing the collar and nipple clamps, and ordered her to lay on her side. As soon as she did so, the guys climbed onto the bed with her. Vasco was behind her. Ty, in front, was already playing with her pussy, while occasionally tugging on the nipple clamps.

She cried out when Vasco's fingers gently probed her pleasantly sore ass.

"You left stripe marks over her backside, Ty," he said. "It sure does look pretty."

"She's too damned tempting," Ty replied, sliding down the bed and applying his lips to her cunt.

Sorrel cried out and almost elevated from the bed. Vasco's large hand on her hip kept her pinned to the mattress.

"Easy, sugar. Let Ty have a little drink of your sweet honey."

"His tongue. It's wicked," she gasped as pleasure rippled through her from the contact. She didn't want to tell them she had never had this done to her before. Jordi expected her to give him head, but never returned the favor. Well, it had been worth waiting to be serviced by an expert. Bolts of lightning streaked through her blood stream and she felt herself close to orgasm. Again. "Shouldn't be allowed." She gasped.

She was so taken up with what Ty was doing to her that it took her a moment to realize Vasco had slipped the tip of his cock into her backside. She instinctively fought against the intrusion.

"Shush, babe, it'll be okay. You want this, you know you do."

His soothing voice and the feel of his hand softly caressing her buttocks helped her to relax and she quit fighting him. Vasco sank just in a little bit more, sighed, and then withdrew again.

"You like that, darlin'? Want me to fuck you a little deeper?"

"Yes, please, Master."

"Take the edge off, Ty," Vasco said. "Otherwise she won't last five minutes."

It felt as though Ty sucked her entire clit into his mouth, his magical tongue swirling and probing until she cried out and her world imploded. She bucked to a climax in his mouth, groaning and pulsating with renewed need as Vasco continued to gently stroke her ass with his massive cock.

As soon as she regained her senses, everything changed. Ty was flat on his back and Vasco ordered her to lay over him, taking her weight on her arms. She knew what they planned to do, and was both excited and terrified at the same time. She was reassured when it occurred to her that they wouldn't push her past her limits. She trusted them in that respect. Trusted them to know what her limits actually were, since she had no idea.

"Okay, sweet thing," Vasco said, crouching behind her and again swishing her butt with his large, capable hands. "We're gonna fill you with our cocks because you're so damned hot for us, and it's what you want." He paused. "It is what you want, isn't it, sugar? I need to hear you say it."

Was it? "Yes," she said breathlessly. "But I'm scared."

"Don't be," Ty muttered. "We'll take real good care of you."

"Safeword us if it gets too much, honey," Vasco said.

"I will, Masters."

"Good girl. Now then, you need to keep absolutely still, and let us do all the work. Can you do that?"

She swallowed. "I'll try."

"You need to do more than try, sweetness. We don't want to hurt you, or cause any damage."

"Yes, I understand."

"Okay, let's give our little sub what she needs and fuck her senseless, Ty."

"You got it, bud."

Ty eased his twitching, pulsating cock into her, stunning her senses with his smooth fluidity, filling her to capacity with his thick length. There would never be enough room for Vasco, too. They had gotten that part wrong, but she had no breath left to protest. Let them do their worst. She felt the bed dip as Vasco lowered himself over her and one of his arms appeared beside her face—rock-hard biceps and corded muscles standing proud in his forearms. She felt him play with her anus, and then his cock infiltrated. At precisely that moment, Ty withdrew, making space for him. How did he know when to do that? Practice, she figured, trying not to feel jealous when she imagined all the faceless females they had honed their skills on. All that mattered was that they were doing it to her now. Her anxiety had fallen away in the face of their smooth expertise and she surrendered herself to their skilful care.

"That's it, babe. Relax and let us give you pleasure," Vasco said, easing a little further into her, and then withdrawing.

It was Ty's turn to thrust into her and he did so with considerable vigor, presumably because it wasn't necessary for him to take as much care as Vas was doing. Then they reversed the procedure again, Vasco going a little deeper this time. But not deep enough. The desire to push back against him became increasingly difficult to resist, but she recalled what Vasco had said about doing damage and restrained herself.

"You okay?" Ty asked.

"Yes. This is…well, it's just—"

"We know," Vasco said chuckling, presumably at her verbal ineptitude. He had a point, but she would defy any woman to speak coherently when surrounded by all that virile masculinity, and filled with two such huge cocks. "Come on, buddy, let's not keep the lady waiting."

They picked up their rhythm like a well-oiled machine, driving in and out of her in perfect synchronization until she thought she might well lose her mind. She was so glad Ty had sucked an orgasm out of her before this started. Otherwise she would have come at once and probably rejected Vasco fucking her ass because she would have felt too sensitive to withstand it. They knew that. Of course they did. Even so, she felt another orgasm building at quite an alarming rate, far too quickly, surely. She figured they had meant this to go on for a while yet, and would be angry with her for her lack of restraint. That was hardly her fault. She couldn't be held responsible for the way her body responded to their dual assault upon it.

"Okay, darlin'." Vasco tapped her butt hard. "We feel your need. Let it go, sweet thing. Come for us."

Sorrel didn't need inviting twice. She deliberately moved her head so the nipple clamps bit, Vasco drove a little harder and a little deeper into her ass, and she exploded. She cried out their names, no longer caring if she moved as she thrashed against one large cock, then the other, thinking she would never get enough of them.

"That's it, boys. Give me more. Shit, that's deep."

The pleasure was so intense that she barely felt the burning sensation in her ass as moans fired her lust and she rode the crescendo of the most powerful, prolonged orgasm she had ever experienced. She opened her eyes wide, staring at Ty in bald stupefaction as on and on it went, wild sensations fragmenting her senses, swamping all reason.

"That's it, babe, take what you need," Vasco muttered from behind, his hot, heavy breath peppering her skin.

And that was what the guys then did. They exploded almost in unison, just as they had done everything else that night, flooding her with a torrent of sperm.

They withdrew, removed the clamps and the three of them lay side by side for several minutes, too boneless to move. They were bathed in thin films of perspiration and were all smiling like imbeciles.

"Wow," Vasco said, lightly touching her belly, which she instinctively sucked in. "That was something else. You okay, darlin'?"

"Okay?" She widened her eyes. "How can you ask such a dumb question? I had absolutely no idea anything like that was possible."

"It's never been that good for us, either," Ty said softly.

"Come on," Vasco said, levering himself from the bed and reaching out a hand to her. "We'll get cold laying here like this. Besides, we need to get clean."

They did just that. Then Ty went down to close up and took Marley out. When he came back he suggested a session in the steam room.

"Good idea," Vasco said. "It'll help ease the aches in your muscles, darlin'."

Sorrel had never set foot in a steam room before, but this seemed to be a night for firsts.

"You're right," she said, snuggled up between them on the bench, breathing in the aromatic steam deep into her lungs. Her head rested in Vasco's lap, her feet, predictably, in Ty's. "This feels *sooo* good."

"Wait until you see what comes next," Ty said, grinning. Well, she thought he grinned. It was hard to be sure, what with all that steam. But she was suspicious. What were they plotting now?

She wasn't left in ignorance for long. They left the steam room and she was ushered into what looked like a circular shower. Except it was an ice room, but she didn't find that out until it was too late. The floor was freezing and ice water dripped down on her. She squealed and tried to back out, but two hunky bodies blocked her path.

"It's therapeutic. Once round and you can come out again," they said, following right behind her. "You'll thank us afterward."

"Don't count on it," Sorrel replied, her teeth chattering.

But strangely enough, it worked. She took another warm shower once she was allowed to escape the freezing cold and her body felt rejuvenated. All her aches and pains had dissolved and she snuggled into bed that night, sandwiched between their hot bodies, feeling more in control of her life than she had for years.

"You'll have to tell me where to go to get more of the same," she said sleepily.

"What?" they demanded in unison.

"Well, when I go back home. You think I can live without what you've opened my eyes to? There are clubs for this sort of thing, aren't there?"

She sensed rather than observed something dark pass between them and wondered what she'd done wrong. Perhaps she'd imagined it, was seeing ghosts where none existed. She shook off the feeling, glad to discover she was no longer suspicious about their motives and could speak her mind freely. They had looked after her throughout the marathon sexfest, opening her eyes to the person she was supposed to be. She felt as though she had graduated sex school with honors, for which they ought to take the credit.

They had no ulterior motive. She had nothing to worry about. They had recognized in her a kindred spirit—one who could be relied upon to keep quiet about their lifestyle and not use insider knowledge to try and carve out a permanent niche in their lives. She had seen the hunger in the eyes of more than one slim young thing in the gym whenever one of the guys appeared. Sorrel didn't mind that her appearance made her seem like a safe bet to her gorgeous Adonises. She would simply make the most of her time with them and leave here knowing a whole lot more about hot, kinky sex than she had when she'd arrived.

How bad could that be?

But there was just one problem. Despite the way she'd behaved with the guys, she never had been one to enter into casual sexual relationships, hence her lack of experience. She didn't think she could get by without more of the same, now that the guys had opened her eyes to what she'd been missing out on. But nor could she imagine doing those things with anyone other than the two hot studs between whom she was currently snuggled.

Especially since she'd fallen headfirst in love with them both.

But that, Sorrel decided, as her eyes fluttered to a close, was information best kept to herself.

Chapter Thirteen

Mid-morning the following day, Vasco and Ty briefly hooked up between classes. They watched one of their trainers and an intern putting the boot camp victims through a hard session of cross-training.

"They're shaping up okay," Vasco remarked. "And we've had less dropouts than I anticipated."

Ty chuckled. "I think they're shit-scared of Lauren."

Vasco shuddered. "They ain't the only ones."

"I heard one of them talking about dropping out the other day, and Lauren near bit his head off. She told him not be such a wuss, and that a little pain was good for the soul, to say nothing of the waistline."

"Who knew Lauren would become our champion?" Vasco grinned. "Did she hit on you yesterday?"

"She hits on me every chance she gets, but I think that's just the way she is. If either of us took her up on her invitation, she'd probably turn tail and run."

"Don't know about you, bud, but I'm not up for taking the chance."

"I hear you, bro."

Lauren saw them watching and blew them a kiss. Vasco couldn't help laughing as he waved back.

"Let's hope she brings the corporate membership home to roost, otherwise we are in deep shit, like you didn't already know it." Vasco ran a hand through his hair, exasperated. "As things stand, we're gonna struggle to make next month's rent."

"I hear you, buddy." Ty sighed. "But never lose sight of the fact that we do have one alternative."

"I know, but I'd prefer not to go down that route."

"Me neither, but it's good to know we have a safety net."

"Seen Sorrel this morning?" Vasco asked in an abrupt change of subject. "She was dead to the world when I got up, poor baby. We wore her out."

"She wasn't complaining."

Vasco grinned. "No, but I hope we didn't take her too far too fast. We have a duty of care."

"It's hard not to push ahead when faced with her sort of enthusiasm." Ty chuckled. "Her face when she thought you were gonna take that butt plug away from her."

"Shit, Ty, just thinking about her makes me so fucking hard."

"Yeah, it's getting embarrassing. I need to carry something around with me all the time to cover the evidence." Ty pulled a rueful expression. "Anyway, I went up a while ago and she and Marley weren't there. I figure they must have gone out for a walk."

"She's really taken to the lifestyle." Vasco sounded as proud as he felt. "I just knew she was a natural the first moment I saw her. Shit, every time of think of you flogging her cute butt, of her bringing herself off in the park, of the way she let us both fuck her when she'd never been ass-fucked before…hell, I've been walking around with a near permanent hard-on since meeting her."

"You and me both, brother." Ty waved in the direction of his jutting cock. "You and me both."

"So, what are we gonna do about her? She won't give up on the life now that she's discovered what she's been missing, but I'm damned if I'll let her go off and offer herself as a sub at some sleazy BDSM club." Vasco scowled as he recalled her casually phrased question on the subject last night. "She'll be taken advantage of. Not all of those joints are reputable."

"Yeah, the same thought had occurred to me, but we don't have a lot of time to decide what we're gonna do. It's Saturday tomorrow," Ty pointed out. "We said we'd take her back to her apartment to see who's been stealing her slogans."

"And she'll assume she's gonna stay." Vasco grimaced. "Can't let that happen. If she wants to play sex games she can damned well play them with us. We've got more than enough cock between us to keep even her satisfied."

"Ah, so you're thinking the unthinkable, too."

"Yeah, I guess so. She's special. The hot babe we didn't realize we'd been looking for. We'd be idiots to let her go."

"You're suggesting we ask her to move in here with us?" Ty asked, raising one brow in astonishment. Vasco had good reasons for not doing commitment.

"Yeah, I guess so. I've gotten used to having her around, and I kinda like it."

"I thought I'd feel threatened by a permanent presence, like I was losing my independence. But having Sorrel here makes me feel...I dunno, complete I guess."

"You know how I feel about all that shit, but...say, who's that with Jenner?"

Vasco and Ty looked down from the second floor balcony where they were standing. "Couple of prospective new members, by the looks of things," Ty said, shrugging. No big deal."

"Those women look familiar. Where have I seen them before?"

"And awful interested in us," Ty added when they glanced up at them and were slow to look away again.

"We'd best go and play nice," Vasco said. "Can't afford to turn our back on two membership fees."

Before they could do so, Sorrel sailed through the front door, Marley tucked under her arm. She saw the guys and a huge smile broke out across her face. It faded fast when she saw the two women with Jenner.

"Mom, Maggie," she said. "What are you two doing here?"

"Shit!" Vasco thumped his clenched fist against the railing. "This can only mean trouble for our babe."

* * * *

"Hello, darling," Mom said. "What a lovely surprise. This young lady was just showing us the facilities."

"You don't live around here," Sorrel replied, narrowing her eyes at them both.

"Nor do you," Maggie answered. "But you're here."

Jenner glanced between them, probably sensing the tension. Definitely looking embarrassed. "Why don't I leave you guys alone for a minute?" she suggested.

"Thanks, Jenner," Sorrel replied. "That would probably be best."

"I assume this is no coincidence," Sorrel said in a mordent tone once Jenner left them. "How did you find me and what do you want?"

"Good morning to you, too, sister dear."

"I saw a café across the street," Mom replied at the same time. "Why don't we go and get a coffee?"

Sorrel was furious, and didn't want to go anywhere with her family. But she could also see they were attracting unwanted attention and thought it would be better to take this elsewhere. Her mother and Maggie wouldn't leave her in peace until they'd said whatever it was they'd come to say. Besides, she really did want to know how they'd found her. She glanced up at Vasco and Ty, watching from the floor above with concerned expressions. She shrugged and indicated to them that she wouldn't be long.

"Come on then," she said, marching through the street door ahead of them.

They sat at a table outside the café and ordered coffee from a lad who looked too young to shave. Marley jumped up onto Sorrel's lap and her mother tutted her disapproval. She didn't like Marley, and the feeling was reciprocated. Sorrel was starting to think her dog was a good judge of character when a low growl rumbled in his throat.

"Okay," Sorrel said, once a coffee Sorrel didn't want was placed in front of her. "I'll ask you again, how did you find me and what do you want?"

"We were worried about you," Maggie said. "You were seen dining with two strange men, then disappeared without a word. What were we supposed to think?"

"I spoke to Mom yesterday. She knew I was taking a vacation."

"In a gym?" Maggie ran her eyes down Sorrel's body, looking skeptical. "You hate exercise."

Sorrel suppressed a grin. If only they knew. But she said nothing, knowing one of them would fill the silence.

"Are they the men you were at Dynasty with?" Mom asked. "The two standing in there on the balcony. I gather they own the gym."

"You still haven't told me how you found me?"

"Pete was worried to see you with strangers," Mom replied. "They paid for that meal with a business credit card—"

"And you had Jordi give out that information?" Sorrel couldn't remember the last time she'd been so angry. "You had no right to ask him, and he had no right to pry. The guys could sue."

"Oh, they won't do that. They're more interested in fleecing you," Maggie said. "Honestly, Sorrel, you're so naïve, you don't know when you're being played."

Sorrel turned upon her sister, making no attempt to mask her expression of unmitigated dislike. "Look around this table," she said sweetly. "I've had plenty of experience at being fleeced."

"We're your family," Mom said, placing a hand over Sorrel's. "We have a right to expect your help."

"Really?" Sorrel elevated one brow. "I obviously didn't get that memo."

"Dad left you way more money than any of us got," Maggie said petulantly. "And you don't have kids to think about."

"God, listen to yourselves." Sorrel sighed. "You got a very fair settlement in your divorce, Mom. If you've let it slip through your fingers, then that's hardly my fault."

Mom looked down at her perfect manicure. "You've changed, gotten hard, Sorrel."

"Because I don't give in to emotional blackmail anymore? Get used to it. And as for you and Pete, Maggie, Dad divided his estate equally between the three of us, but you guys took yours way back, whereas mine's remained invested and earned good dividends. That's why I got more."

"Yes," Maggie replied, her eyes lit by spite. "But a fool and her money are soon parted, Sorrel, and if you think those two hunks are interested in you for any other reason, then you're deluded. They are fine-looking men, and they must have women crawling out of the woodwork to get a piece of them. Why would they look twice at you, if not for your money?"

"Maggie!" Mom said sharply.

"She needs to hear the truth, Mom. It's for her own good."

"I don't have to listen to this." Sorrel threw a few bills on the table to cover their check. "Just leave me alone. I don't think we have anything else to say to one another."

"Sorrel," Mom said. "I know you don't want to hear it because I can tell from your face that you've been having some fun, and I'm glad for you. Really I am. But you ought to know the two guys you've become friendly with *are* in financial difficulties. They're late with their payments to their bank and behind on their rent for the gym."

Sorrel felt color drain from her face. "No," she said softly.

"I'm sorry, darling, but it's true. Pete made a few calls. It was easy to find out."

"They haven't once asked me how much I inherited," she said slowly. "They haven't shown any interest in my money at all," she added, almost to herself.

"They're professional leeches. They know better than to be so obvious. And as to knowing how much, the will's been probated," Maggie said, "so it's a matter of public record."

All Sorrel's doubts came flooding back, but she pushed them aside, refusing to believe her mother and sister had gotten it right. Not everyone operated the same way those two grasping opportunists did. She would talk to the guys, ask them straight out about their business finances, and would know from their responses if they were out to use her, just like everyone else connected with her appeared to be.

"Come back to Seattle with us, darling," Mom said. "I hate to think of you being exploited. We'll look after you. We're your family."

"No, thanks. I have things to do here." She stood up. "I'll be back soon. I'll call you when I am." *Perhaps.*

Sorrel couldn't stay with her family a moment longer. Her mother's fake concern, her sister's open spite, was unendurable. She knew the guys were struggling to make ends meet—the telephone conversation she overheard Vasco make, the overdue bills, their desperate need to procure a corporate membership—but she hadn't once thought they planned to ask her for a hand out. She still refused to believe it. She knew them better than that. They weren't like her family.

They absolutely were not.

She darted back across the road, then slowed her pace, struggling to get her emotions under control before she re-entered the gym. Jenner waved to her when she walked through the door.

"The guys are in the office, if you're looking for them," she said. "They said to go on up."

"Thanks, Jenner."

On the point of entering the office, she heard them talking and the nature of their conversation stopped her in her tracks.

"It's no good." She heard Vasco shuffling some papers and sighing. "Whichever way we come at it, the numbers just don't add up."

"So, you'll approach her?"

"We have no choice. I didn't want to go down that route, but if we want to save the gym, I can't think of any other way."

Sorrel choked on a sob. So it was true. Mom had gotten it right. Fury and despondency waged war inside of her. She had never felt so bereft in her entire life. She couldn't talk to them now and dashed up the staircase to the apartment instead, squeezing Marley so tightly beneath her arm that he yelped. Tears streamed down her face, and she felt physically and emotionally drained. What a fool she'd been! When would she learn? Hadn't life already taught her that when something seemed too good to be true, it almost always was?

Well, that was it. She'd pack her stuff up and get a cab back to Seattle. There was nothing left for her here. And there was no point in talking to the guys about it. What was there to say? If they'd wanted money, why the hell didn't they come right out and say so, she wondered, throwing her possessions haphazardly into her bag. They knew how she felt about her appearance, how little self-confidence she had. Why boost her up, just to let her down again?

Ah, of course. They wanted to make her fully dependent upon them before coming out with their request, making it that much harder for her to turn them down. She should have seen that one coming, but they were pretty damned good at what they did. She'd give them that. Their methods of distraction were in a class of their own.

The tears turned into a torrent, blinding her vision. She wiped them impatiently and rather inelegantly away with the sleeve of her sweater, calling herself all kinds of fool, too miserable at first to realize she was no longer alone. She gasped when she sensed two muscular bodies leaning against the door jamb, looking convincingly concerned.

"Babe," Vasco said, reaching for her. "What's wrong? What the hell did they say to you?"

Chapter Fourteen

"Don't touch me!"

Vasco was taken aback by the force of the anger blazing from her eyes, and very concerned by it, but he respected her wishes and didn't try to touch her. Instead he exchanged a glance with Ty, who shrugged, equally thrown by her reaction.

"Where are you going?" Vasco asked, pointing to her half-packed bag.

"Back home," she replied shortly. "I'm done here."

"Mind telling us why?" Ty asked.

"Like you don't already know." She scowled at them as she continued to throw things into her bag. "I'm not quite the trusting idiot you take me for."

"Come again?" Vasco said, frowning.

"I thought we were going back to Seattle together tomorrow," Ty said. "To check on the camera."

"It doesn't matter. I'm going back today, by cab. Right this minute."

"At least tell us what we've done," Vasco said, starting to feel a little annoyed. "Do us that courtesy."

"All right, if you want to play it that way." Her eyes continued to radiate hostility as she stomped past them into the main room. The guys shared a shrug and followed her. "Why didn't you tell me the gym's losing money?"

Vasco just stared at her. All sorts of scenarios had run through his head that might account for her mood. He knew she must be pretty pissed at her family for stalking her, and wondered what they'd said to make her so mad at them. Their finances hadn't figured amongst his cogitations.

"We're struggling," he admitted. "It's a new venture, there's lots of competition which doesn't fight fair, but—"

"But, you stumbled upon me, and I was so pathetically grateful to be noticed by you studs that it stands to reason I'll bail you out."

Ty's fixed her with an angry glare. "Just a goddamned minute—"

"Is that what you really think this is about?" Vasco asked at the same time, pointing in the direction of the bedroom they'd used for their games the night before. "You think we used you for financial reasons?" He shook his head and ran a hand through his hair. "Jesus. You don't have a very high opinion of us."

"What else am I supposed to think? I've seen the way all those slim young things chase after you. I couldn't figure why you'd preferred me when you have hot- and cold-running babes on tap. Now it's starting to make sense."

"If that's what you think then I'll help you pack, while Ty calls you a cab," Vasco said, striding furiously towards her room.

"I heard you just now, in the office, talking about approaching *her* and asking for money," Sorrel threw back at him, pointing a finger at his admittedly gorgeous chest. "So you have no business claiming the moral high ground. You don't have to be a genius to figure out who *she* has to be."

"Is that right?" Vasco fixed her with a scathing look. "You think it was you?"

"Who else could it be?"

"Darlin', even if we were the low lives you seem to think we are, the few hundred thousand bucks, or however much it is that you inherited, wouldn't begin to fix our problems."

"You must know—"

"You might as well tell her, Vas," Ty said, glowering at Sorrel. "If she really thinks we're capable of using her like that then she ain't the person we thought she was. Still, and all, there's no harm in telling her the truth, just so she knows. But it's your call."

* * * *

Sorrel felt the full force of their blistering glares and had a terrible feeling she'd jumped to the wrong conclusion. But that was wishful thinking, surely. Except, why would they be so angry with her if she'd gotten it right. They'd be more likely to use sweet words and their magical hands to talk her around, wouldn't they? In spite of her doubts, or perhaps because of them, she couldn't stay and listen to their excuses.

"I'll wait for the cab downstairs," she said, zipping up her bag and hoisting it over her shoulder. "You don't need to worry about the camera you set up at my place. Now I know it's someone close to me, I'll have the locks changed and be more careful about what I leave lying around. Send me your bill and I'll write you a check. Come on, Marley."

The dog hesitated, whined, then trotted after her, tail between his legs. Hell, this didn't feel right but what else could she do? *Call me back, guys. Make me understand.* She sensed them watching her, still radiating hostility, as she struggled down the stairs with her bags. She ignored the startled looks she received from the people in the gym, tears blurring her vision as she pushed through the front doors. Jenner called out to her, but she couldn't allow herself to be distracted and simply waved over her shoulder without turning back.

She sat in the cab and sobbed all the way back to Seattle. But by the time she was inside her apartment she was all cried out, and had hardened her heart. She'd made a mistake, but she would get over it—get over them—somehow. It had been fun while it lasted, she reminded herself. She was grateful for the introduction to their lifestyle and would definitely check out clubs in the area to see if she could get more of the same—but with no strings attached this time.

Sorrel took Marley for a long walk, returned home and hit the shower, standing under the hot jets for a long time, trying to decide where she went from here. To her astonishment, she wasn't hungry. That had to be a first. She managed a mirthless smile. Perhaps she ought to market the broken-heart diet. It would be a surefire success.

There was something niggling at the back of her mind. Something one of them had said that was significant. She sat up a little straighter when it finally dawned on her. Vasco said something about her inheriting a few hundred thousand. He sounded as though he genuinely thought that was all she had gotten. Could it really be…

The sound of the doorbell startled her. She briefly considered not answering it, but Marley started barking so whoever it was would know she was home. Hope briefly flared. Could the guys have come after her? If they had, she would probably buy into whatever story they'd concocted because, much as she tried to tell herself otherwise, she was addicted to them.

Her face fell when she opened the door and Jordi stood on the threshold.

"Hey, you're back," he said, pushing past her without being invited inside. Marley tried to bite his ankle. Jordi swore and shook the dog off. "What's his problem?"

"If I had to guess, I'd say it was you." Sorrel folded her arms beneath her breasts, in no mood for this encounter. "What do you want?"

"I was worried about you, babe. You appeared in the restaurant with two strange men, then disappeared and weren't taking calls. Anything could have happened to you. You don't seem to realize that you'll be a target for just about every fortune hunter on the planet now that you're rich. You need protecting."

Goddamn it, the man had more front than Macy's. "And you're the one to do the protecting, I suppose?" She held up a hand to prevent him from answering her. "Has it not occurred to you that I might be able to attract a man just because of who I am, not what's in my bank account?"

"Sure." He shrugged. "I was attracted to you. I still am."

"Oh, Jordi." Sorrel shook her head. "Not only did you dump me as soon as your career took off, but your timing sucked. My dad had just been blown to smithereens. You knew how much he meant to me, I needed you, and you weren't there for me." She turned away from him. "I can never forgive you for that."

He tried to touch her, but she shook him off. "I'm sorry, darlin', I was wrong, I can see that now. I guess success went to my head for a while."

Sorrel shot him a look. "You think?"

"It's not been the same without you. I miss you so damned much, and it took seeing you with other guys to make me realize it. Can't we give it another go? I want you, not your money. I always have, deep down. There's a connection between us that I can't get past. I don't want to get past it."

He seemed sincere, but even if he was, Sorrel wasn't playing ball. A few short weeks ago she probably would have given him the benefit of the doubt and taken him back. But she was no longer that person, and her brief encounter with the guys had given her a little, a very little, self-belief. She could make her own way, without a permanent man—or men—in her life, and that was what she intended to do.

"I think you'd better leave, Jordi," she said, opening the door for him. "Thanks for stopping by."

He hesitated on the threshold, looking despondent, because she'd rejected him and his ego had taken a hit, or because he now accepted her money wouldn't ever be his? "If you change your mind, I'll be waiting."

Chapter Fifteen

Sorrel actually took her landline off the hook and switched off her cell phone after two calls from her brother and one from her mother. It was the only way to stop her family hounding her. She then opened a bottle of wine had drowned her sorrows. She woke the following morning with a slight headache, feeling bereft but still determined to maintain her independence. She took Marley for an hour's walk, twice the length she would once have attempted, and felt her head gradually clearing.

Her heart lifted when she returned to the apartment and saw the distinctive figures of Vasco and Ty waiting on her doorstep. They looked serious, unreachable, whereas she couldn't seem to help smiling. Marley broke the tension by hurling himself at them, wagging his entire body and yapping with pleasure. Sorrel had a hard time not following his example.

"Hey," she said, because someone had to say something. "Did you come for the camera?"

Vasco scowled. "Not precisely."

"I guess you'd better come in."

"*She* is Mrs. Gladstone," Vasco said without preamble as soon as they followed her into the apartment.

Sorrel, in the process of filling the kettle, turned to look at him. "I beg your pardon."

"You heard us referring to a woman who might help us with funding. We were referring to Mrs. Gladstone. You met her yesterday after the seniors' class."

"Oh." Sorrel clapped a hand over her mouth.

"*Oh* about covers it." Vasco's voice was tight with controlled anger. In fact, he looked so rigid he kind of frightened her. "She's loaded, but comes to Body Language instead of going to the classier gyms in the city because she says they're pretentious and don't cater for older members in the way we do. She got wind of the fact that we were struggling and offered to become a sleeping partner in the business. We're reluctant because we don't know yet if we can make it work and don't want her to throw her money away."

"Why…why would she make an offer like that?"

"Because her granddaughter was attacked," Ty said. "She now attends Vasco's defense classes and Mrs. G. is grateful that she's learned how to look out for herself."

"Oh, shit." Sorrel sat down, shaking her head. "I'm so sorry. Looks like I got it wrong."

"Yeah, you did." Vasco drilled her with a look. "How could you think we'd do that to you, especially after all the stuff we've enjoyed together?"

"I don't know." She shrugged. "I'm sorry, I guess I'm used to being exploited and kinda expect it of people."

"Darlin', it would take more than the few thousand you inherited from your dad to sort this place out," Ty said. "In order to compete with the others, we need to purchase the derelict building next door, put in a full-sized pool, link the two buildings, put in an outdoor training circuit, a café…need I spell it out?"

"The other gyms in the area offer those facilities?"

"Yeah, but right now we're more interested in attracting members, keeping our heads above water, and building a reputation."

"Hence your need for the corporate membership deal?"

"Right."

Sorrel frowned. "You always seem to be quite busy. Why isn't it paying off?"

"Because we've had to cut membership fees to a minimum to compete with the others. They can afford to cut their fees because they're established, and that's what they've done to try and put us out of business," Vasco explained.

"But the boot camp, the seniors, the defense classes—all those things must help."

"The boot camp is too new to have much effect on the bottom line yet," Ty replied. "We only charge the seniors a small fee because a lot of them wouldn't be able to come otherwise, same with the defense classes."

"The seniors I understand, but why do the defense classes if they don't pay? That's not good business practice."

She noticed Ty look pointedly at Vasco. No one spoke and the atmosphere was rife with tension. Even Marley appeared to sense it. He whined, and took himself off to a corner where he curled up on a rug. Sorrel felt terrible for doubting them, and worse about spoiling what they'd had going. She should have kept faith in the guys and not taken what she'd overheard at face value. There was always more than one explanation for everything. Besides, her Mom and Maggie were hardly upstanding examples of incorruptibility. Of course they would assume the worst of the guys, because they judged everyone by their own standards. Besides, it suited them to ensure Sorrel distanced herself from them and put herself back within their grasping…well, grasps. It all seemed so obvious now, but then hindsight was a wondrous thing. Now, she had lost the guys' faith and was unsure if she deserved to get it back again.

"You asked me once about my family," Vasco said, his voice jolting her out of her self-hatred wallow, "and I didn't really give you an answer. That's because I never talk about them. Ever. But I'll tell you, just so you know I'm not the heartless bastard you seem to think I am."

"Vas, I never meant to—"

"My family were, and probably still are, well off high-achievers. I wouldn't know. I've cut off all contact. My dad's a top defense attorney, Mom's a successful interior designer. We don't do failure in my family," he said with a cynical twist to his lips. "And we don't do less than perfect." He paused, staring off into the distance, some place where she wouldn't have been able to reach him even if she hadn't lost his trust. "I had a sister five years younger than me." He turned to face her, fixing her with a look of eerie fervency. "A sister who was a lot like you."

"Was?" Sorrel asked breathlessly.

"She developed early, was embarrassed by her breasts and the fact that she was a little overweight. That, of course, was unacceptable in our perfect family unit, and Mom and Dad never let her lose sight of the fact."

"And so she comfort ate," Sorrel said softly, nodding in understanding.

"Yeah, she did, but instead of helping her through that hard time, Mom in particular was on her case the entire time. Dad largely ignored her. I graduated high school, refused to go to an Ivy League college and follow in the family tradition, and enlisted instead. My father turned his back on me from that day onwards. In fact, the only person I kept in touch with was Alice, my sister. I knew she was miserable, being teased by the other kids, getting no support at home. I should have fucking been there for her when she had no one else." His expression was agonized, full of guilt and self-disgust. "But I was too busy rebelling against the old man, and the world in general, to realize just how bad the situation had gotten."

He smashed his fist against the wall, and Sorrel saw tears in his eyes. She longed to comfort him but knew he would reject the gesture. She glanced at Ty and he shook his head, as though understanding her need and warning her off.

"She was attacked one night, raped—"

"Oh my God!" This time Sorrel did stand up, reach out and touch his arm. She was unsure if he even noticed. He was still in a place where she couldn't get to him. "She survived the attack but was never the same again. Six months later she took an overdose and killed herself."

"That is so tragic." Fresh tears poured down Sorrel's face. "No wonder it's so important for you to help girls protect themselves. If someone had done that for Alice then—"

"Yeah." Vasco finally looked at her. "When we met you, your insecurities reminded me of Alice, and I knew there was a person in there worth getting to know. Or so I thought. Looks like I got that wrong."

"You weren't wrong, Vasco." She risked reaching for his hand and lacing her fingers with his. "But if you know anything about how Alice reacted to kindness, then you might be able to see how I felt when Mom told me you were hurting financially and were out to manipulate me. I was like Alice, invisible to a beautiful world, until I came into money. Then, all of a sudden, everyone wanted a piece of me."

"Except the jerk," Ty pointed out.

"Oh, he didn't know at the time how much I'd gotten. Just as soon as the will was probated and it became public knowledge, he hooked up with my brother again, but Pete's too stupid to realize why he did that. He's flattered that a celebrity chef wants to go into business with him."

"Definitely a jerk," Vasco muttered.

Sorrel thought of the way he'd been the night before when he called round—contrite and genuine-seeming. She was glad he'd come because it proved to her that she really was over him. These two were another matter. Were they here, explaining when they didn't need to, because they still wanted her? Hope flared.

"I didn't want to believe it about you guys." She encompassed them both with her gaze. "I didn't believe it, until I overheard you talking in the office. I jumped to the wrong conclusion. I'm so very sorry." She wiped away her tears. "I've spoiled what we could have had together, haven't I?" Neither of them spoke, which was all the answer she required.

"We still want you, but not your fucking money." Vasco actually smiled when his voice finally cut through the brittle silence, and Sorrel couldn't recall ever seeing a more beautiful sight. "We were going to ask you if you'd consider staying, moving in with us permanently."

Sorrel blinked, unsure if he'd actually said the words she had forfeited the right to hear by not trusting them.

"You…er, want me?" She swallowed. "Just for who I am?"

"We love you," Ty said simply. "We didn't see that one coming but we're mighty glad it did."

A slow smile spread across her lips. "Love? Me?" She shook her head, convinced she had to be hearing voices. "Are you absolutely sure about that?"

"How can I stay mad at her when she's so fucking adorable?" Vasco asked, pulling her into his arms. "We were hooked on our feelings for you, almost from the first. You, not your money. When are we gonna get it through your head that we want you for who you are, darlin'? Your few thousand bucks won't make a dent in our plans."

"Actually," she replied, happiness fizzing through her blood stream. "They very well might. I love you both, too. I thought I was being greedy as well as unrealistic because I couldn't choose between you."

"Nope," Ty said, extracting her from Vasco's arms and sliding his hands possessively over her buttocks. "That's the way it works in our world. Two into one definitely goes."

"I do have one condition of my own though."

"Name it," they said together.

"I want to become your sleeping partner, literally and in a business sense."

"That's real sweet of you, sugar," Vasco replied. "But like we already told you—"

"You don't seem to understand," she said, cutting him off in her haste to make him do so. "I didn't inherit a few hundred thousand." She paused, grinning at them both. "I inherited close to two million."

"You what!" Vasco's mouth fell open and he sank onto the settee. "You have got to be kidding us."

"No wonder your family have been hounding you," Ty added, also falling onto the couch.

"Nope. I've been looking for a good investment opportunity," she said, sitting between them and placing a hand on each of their thighs. "What say you we give those other local gyms a run for their money…er, using my money to do it?"

"Darlin', we couldn't do that," Vasco said.

"Why not? Mind you, I ought to tell you, I'm a tough negotiator, and I shall expect a high return on my investment."

"How much do you have in mind?" Ty asked warily.

"Oh, I don't know." She bit her lower lip as she pretended to think about it. "Shall we say, hot sex at least twice a day for the next twenty…no, make it thirty years?"

"Baby," they replied with one voice. "You've got yourself a deal."

They sealed that deal in the bedroom, which took a considerable amount of time. They were nothing if not thorough, Sorrel thought happily, as she lay spread-eagled and blindfolded, her hands fastened to the headboard by one of her scarves while Ty sucked her clit and Vasco played with her backside.

"How soon can you move in with us?" he asked.

"How about today?"

He chuckled. "Take all the time you need."

"We've wasted enough time."

"Amen to that, darlin'."

Then Vasco slid his huge cock into her backside while Ty sucked the first of several orgasms from her and coherent thought became impossible. Instead she devoted all her energy into begging and pleading with them to give her more—always more. They were more than happy to oblige.

"Stay right where you are, sweet thing," Ty said when they finally ran out of stamina. "I'm gonna check that camera and find out who the thief was. I want to know, even if you don't."

"My money's on the sister," Vasco said, remaining right where he was, lazily running his fingers over one of Sorrel's sensitized breasts while she used his broad shoulder as a pillow.

"Shit, I hate it when he's right," Ty said, returning a short time later with the camera in hand, showing a clear picture of Maggie going through the papers Sorrel had left on the table.

"I'm not surprised," Sorrel said, sighing. "But I'm glad I know for sure. It will make it easier to cut off all relations with her and her spoiled kids."

"You don't plan to confront her?" Vasco asked.

"Only if she comes after me for more money. Otherwise, I don't see the point."

"Yeah," Ty agreed. "That's probably best. You can't choose your families, darlin', and no one says you have to like them."

"Just as well," Sorrel replied, screwing up her nose.

"Come on, gorgeous," Vasco said, pulling her to her feet. "Let's get showered. Then we'll help you pack up your stuff and close this place up."

* * * *

"Vasco and Tyler got to the bottom of Sorrel's problems," Raoul said, hanging up the phone and chuckling.

"Yeah." Zeke looked up from his laptop. "Who was it then?"

"Turns out it was her sister. She felt hard done by because Sorrel inherited a shedload of dosh from their old man and she felt she didn't get her fair share. Seems she did, but she conveniently forgot about it."

"Charming."

"Yeah well, Vas and Tyler think so. Sorrel's moved in with them and put her money into the gym."

Zeke's mood brightened. "That's good. I'm glad someone's got a happy ever after."

"Sounds to me like Sorrel deserves it. The guys sure as hell do. They've worked their asses off to make that gym a success."

"Who'd have thought Sorrel's own family would shaft her like that." Zeke rolled his eyes. "Aren't families supposed to look out for each other?"

"Yeah well, we'll never get to know, will we?" Raoul replied, moodily.

Tomorrow was the third anniversary of Cantara's death. They didn't talk about it, but both dreaded it. It was a day for renewed recriminations. A day to be endured, just like all the ones that had preceded it over the past three years.

They both knew they'd never feel that way about another woman ever again, and couldn't seem to put the past behind them, no matter how hard they tried. And they sure as hell had tried. It did no good. Even if they found a woman they liked, Cantara's memory haunted them, dooming the relationship before it got off the ground. Much as their own guilt at being unable to save her ate away at them like a virulent disease. They should have trusted their instincts and never let her to go in the first place. They had known it was too dangerous. Hell, if Raoul could have his time over…

"Come on, buddy," Zeke said, reaching for a bottle of bourbon and two glasses. "If ever an occasion called for getting wasted, this is it."

"Amen to that."

They raised their glasses in a silent toast to Cantara's memory, Raoul still able to vividly recall her beautiful face and piercing green eyes, the sound of her musical laughter, and intensity of her lovely smile.

"Come back to us, babe," Raoul whispered, tears pricking the back of his eyes. "We just can't hack it without you."

THE END

WWW.ZARACHASE.COM

ABOUT THE AUTHOR

Zara Chase is a British author who spends a lot of her time travelling the world. Being a gypsy provides her with ample opportunities to scope out exotic locations for her stories. She likes to involve her heroines in her erotic novels in all sorts of dangerous situations—and not only with the hunky heroes whom they encounter along the way. Murder, blackmail, kidnapping and fraud make frequent appearances in her books, adding pace and excitement to her racy stories.

Zara is an animal lover who enjoys keeping fit and is on a one-woman mission to keep the wine industry ahead of the recession.

For all titles by Zara Chase, please visit
www.bookstrand.com/zara-chase

Siren Publishing, Inc.
www.SirenPublishing.com

Lightning Source UK Ltd.
Milton Keynes UK
UKOW06f2156050615

252994UK00016B/283/P

9 781627 419093